Notes on a Marriage

Also by Marie Lavoie (in translation)
Mister Roger and Me

Marie Lavoie

Notes on a Marriage

WELBECK

Published in 2021 by Welbeck Fiction Limited, part of Welbeck Publishing Group
20 Mortimer Street London W1T 3JW

Original Title: Autopsie d'une femme plate par Marie-Renée Lavoie
Copyright © 2017, Les Éditions XYZ inc.
English translation copyright © 2019 by Arielle Aaronson

First published as Autopsie d'une femme plate in 2017 by Les Éditions XYZ inc
First published in English by House of Anansi Press Inc. in 2019
First published by Welbeck Fiction Limited in 2020
This edition published by Welbeck Fiction Limited in 2021

A CIP catalogue record for this book is available from the British Library

ISBN 978-1-78739-469-8

Printed and bound by CPI Group (UK) Ltd., Croydon, CR0 4YY

10 9 8 7 6 5 4 3 2 1

To anyone whose heart has been shattered
by a "forever" cut short.

Because we just have to laugh.

1

In which I give you my thoughts on marriage

I'VE ALWAYS THOUGHT it terribly pretentious to gather all your loved ones in one place in order to say: the two of us, right here, right now, and in spite of the overwhelming statistics, declare that we, temporarily bonded by the illusion of eternity, we are *forever*. And we've asked you to spend time and money to be here today because we – *We* – we shall elude whatever it is that dissolves other loves. Aged twenty-three, we are certain of this and want to share our conviction with you. We're neither convinced nor frightened that the vast majority have stumbled before the implausibility of this oath. Our love will endure because *our* love is special. Our love is not like other people's. Our marriage *will survive*. But at nearly every wedding reception, pretty much all of them drunken affairs, guests flood the dance floor to shout, doing their best to drown out Gloria Gaynor, that they have survived the death of their own illusions. I've seen them, women of a certain age clutching their imaginary microphones and awarding themselves a sense of invincibility as they belt out the only lyrics everyone remembers from the song: *I will survive, hey, hey!* Yes, they survived, despite their divorce. Hey, hey.

All in all, there's really only one problem with marriage, and that's the exchange of vows. You can't take them seriously, these promises to love from this day forward, in sickness and in health, until death do you part. For the sake of being honest with future generations who insist on getting married, I propose we rewrite the script to give it more of a twenty-first-century, less fairy-tale feel: "I solemnly swear to love you, *blah blah blah*, until I stop loving you. Or until I fall for someone else." Because there's no denying it: the steamroller of everyday life is bound to quash even the strongest, most ardent passion.

Sure, everyone knows couples who have been together sixty years through thick and thin, perfect metaphors that for centuries have magnified the distress of spouses held captive by their promises. More children are born with a sixth finger or toe than there are couples who have truly spent a lifetime happy with each other. And yet while having an extra digit is deemed an "exceptional anomaly" by science, marriage remains a bedrock of society. When's the next Sixth Finger Expo?

Me, all I ever wanted was to live with the man of my dreams and have his babies. We would raise them and cherish them, supporting each other as best we could, for as long as we could. I'd have loved my little bastard children so much. And my husband too, even if he'd just stayed my boyfriend. Perhaps I'd have loved even better, free of the girdle of marriage that prevented me from realizing our love had crumbled from within.

I married because my in-laws thought my love was suspiciously simple. Before that, I'd never thought of simplicity as a flaw. They'll have their fill of complexity now. Divorces are never lacking in that department.

I spent years building myself back up after he announced, "I'm leaving, I'm in love with someone else." It wasn't me he killed with those murderous words, but all the notions of myself I'd constructed through his eyes, through the sacred union that completed and defined me. A union to which I'd surrendered myself entirely, seeing as we'd sealed it with holy vows and blessed rings.

When he told me he could no longer keep his promise, I came undone. With just a few words, I lost my bearings. And during that dizzying descent into hell, everything I grabbed for purchase slipped from my fingers.

You might think I resented him for no longer loving me, but you'd be wrong. We can't control our feelings – everyone knows that. And that's a good thing. We might be blinded by anger momentarily, but we all come to terms with it at some point. That was something even I could understand, looking beyond the complete devastation I was enduring. And, besides, how could I have forced him to keep on loving me? Wouldn't he have preferred to still be in love with me? Everyone's lives would have been easier, starting with his own. He wouldn't have needed to explain, apologize, justify, and defend himself to so many people and for such a long time before wishing for a return to peace. To be honest, I never envied him once.

That said, I wanted him to pay for all the marks that time, unforgiving, had left on my body. Though I can't blame him, I'm still bitter that the years did him nothing but favours given today's tastes in men. Male movie stars are even more attractive in their fifties, but you'd nervously piss your pants if you saw Monica Bellucci play a Bond girl. It was for this dirty injustice that I hated my husband, him and his little bimbo, him and the power he had to start over at an age when my reproductive organs were announcing their retirement. Soon I had so much bile in me that I started to hate myself, body and soul. If Jacques had needed a few more reasons to decamp, I could have provided them by the dozen.

Whatever. Like all those other women, I *survived*.

2

In which I sink slowly, dragged down by my own weight

"I'M IN LOVE WITH someone else."

A rush of blood filled my head. My eyes throbbed in their sockets; a few millimetres more and they'd have popped right out. The declaration seemed so absurd that I glanced at the TV, hoping the words came from somewhere else. But the two celebrities trying to stuff a chicken with prosciutto were roaring with laughter. They weren't talking about falling out of love.

"Diane . . . I didn't mean to . . . It's not you, but . . . uuughh . . ."

He launched into a slurry of clichés that tasted like garbage juice. He recited them nervously, obviously anxious to get it over with. I didn't catch much, just a few painful words: "dull," "bored," "passion," and that he'd been thinking about "us" for a long time. Charlotte had just moved out, so I'd not yet had time to contemplate the use of a personal pronoun that excluded the kids. I should have, I know. But I realized this a second too late.

"Diane, I . . . I'm leaving . . ."

Jacques left that same night, to give me time to calm down and think. Twenty-five years of marriage, snuffed out in a few words. He believed it wouldn't be good for me if he stayed; that I needed space to digest the news – admittedly a difficult pill to swallow. I watched his dull, insipid words scatter at my feet and I felt sick to my stomach.

He sighed as he rose, exhausted from all the talk. He didn't want to tell me where he was going, but it was obvious. "Someone Else" was hammering in the first nails of my crucifixion, waiting for him somewhere, waiting for the two of them to celebrate their new life together.

"How old?"

"What?"

"How old is she?"

"Diane, it's not about age . . ."

"I want to know her *fucking* age!"

I could see the answer in his hangdog eyes: you don't want to know, Diane, you don't want to know. But really, what's the big deal?

"It's not what you think . . ."

When the husband of my friend Claudine left her for one of his students, it wasn't what she was thinking either: "She's absolutely brilliant. She's read all of Heidegger!" It wasn't his fault, poor Philippe, that Heidegger had ejaculated all his philosophizing into the robust brain of one of his students, rendering her completely irresistible. Who's Heidegger? *Who cares.* Claudine certainly didn't give two shits about him – she used a collection of his works as kindling for the fire and to line the cats' litter boxes. Over time, the image of the chick with the Heideggerian-phenomenology-loving brain morphed into one of little mounds of turds. We do what we can to make things easier.

I sat alone in the dark living room, staring at the television Jacques had turned off. I could see myself reflected in the screen, slightly distorted, my silhouette motionless, paralyzed. My body was trapped in a yoke of pain and shame that prevented all movement. If I sat there any longer I'd eventually end up disappearing, slowly swallowed up by the couch. It would be nice to disappear that way, without a fuss. I'd never get in the way of anyone's happiness again – me, the boring wife.

The sun rose from the same place it always did. It surprised me. The end of the world seemed to have no effect on the movement of the stars. I would have to carry on, then, when all I wanted to do was roll over and die. So I got up gingerly, carefully bearing weight on legs drained of all life. They'd need to hang in a little longer, too. I'd start by throwing out the couch I'd urinated on in my catalepsy.

I stepped into the shower fully dressed, wishing I could strip away, like my clothes, all that was clinging to me. I watched as the excess dye from my new blazer swirled on the tile floor, mixing with my urine, mascara, saliva, and tears. But the real filth wouldn't budge.

Outside, I threw all the cushions into a haphazard pile on the freshly mowed lawn. Then, with a sledgehammer I found in the basement, I smashed the couch to pieces, investing all the energy I had left. I accidentally made a giant hole in one of the walls, and it felt good. If I hadn't been so tired, I'd have reduced the house to dust.

Jacques called the next day to see if I was feeling any better. He asked me to show respect for our loved ones and play the "everything's tip-top" card as we told the children, our families, our co-workers. And since our twenty-fifth anniversary was coming up and he didn't think it made sense to cancel everything – "I know, I should have thought about it before . . ." – he insisted we keep things civil and spend the evening together. It would be a quiet family night that everyone "expected and deserved." I felt like one of those Indian brides who, on their very own wedding night, are held back from the celebrations, cere-moniously set aside to receive good wishes for a happiness that is excluding them already. I never really understood what value my life had for other people, anyway.

"Can you think about it and get back to me?"

"Uh-huh."

I always hated that, the "get back to me."

Nevertheless, I did what he said and thought about it.

I opted for a simple, modern solution. I created a Face-book profile (with the help of my son Antoine, coaching me over the telephone). Then I spent hours sending friend requests to the four corners of the province and beyond. I started with my in-laws, his sister, all our distant cousins, colleagues, friends, neighbours, acquaintances, enemies, and all the rest. The moment anyone accepted my request, I selected more people from their own lists of friends to make sure I'd not forgotten anyone. Innumerable people commented on my tardy entry to the world of social media, and oh, how suddenly active I was! I "liked" everything: the things people said, and posted, the comments they made – even the ones telling the world they'd played Tetris that morning or who wanted people to know what kind of tea they were drinking. I commented with an enthusiasm that was as genuine as a fake plant is real.

By evening I had accumulated 329 new friends and was still waiting for a hundred or more responses. I sat down to compose my first-ever Facebook status update. If at all possible, a first should stand out, be unforgettable:

DIANE DELAUNAIS • 8 p.m. • 🌏
Oh all-knowing Facebook, can you tell me if I should cancel my 25th anniversary party given that Jacques (my husband) just announced he is leaving me for "Someone Else"? (Sex undetermined, but predictable), Goal: 300 likes by tomorrow. Please share! Now go watch clips of people wiping out in epic fails.

Then I turned off my computer, cell phone, the lights, the television; I locked all the doors (with their chains and other security latches), took a few sleeping pills, and curled up in a ball on the guest bed. I was suffering too much to find pleasure in anything. I wanted the first few days to play out without my involvement. Let people write to each other, call each other, accuse each other, comfort each other, judge him, complain about me, criticize both of us, gasp, be horrified, analyze and gossip about the whole thing without me; I didn't want to be there for the initial awkwardness, the too-loud whispers of "oh-my-God-she-had-no-idea!", the dodged glances, the baffled faces, and hands covering mouths to contain surprise or shock – or satisfaction, who knows.

I wasn't about to parade around in front of whoever, trying to appear like I didn't want to die. I'd seen so many others, often at work, staggering around like zombies, their arms loaded with files, trying to pretend everything was all right. I took a leave of absence as expensive as a twenty-fifth-anniversary reception and dropped everything for as long as was needed to heal. This is possible when you're forty-eight and you have a bunch of vacation days saved up and money in the bank. I flung the news out like a bloody carcass to a pack of hungry dogs and didn't want to resurface until nothing was left but a pile of gristled bones I could pick up without gagging.

I'd hoped the damage I'd caused by hurling such a bomb would dull the pain. But in the end it only made things worse, throwing the tentacles of our relationship back in my face. I'd always thought physical suffering was the worst, but I'd gladly have given birth without an epidural several times over rather than endure this. And I know what I'm talking about.

In the weeks that followed, I refused to see anyone but my children. Clearly, they too were suffering. I let everyone else pound on the door and flood my inbox and voicemail to their heart's content. I deleted everything without reading or listening. I even deactivated my Facebook profile, without reading the 472 comments that had accumulated. I spent days and nights staring at the ceiling, simply trying to understand what had happened. When, finally, I fell into an exhausted slumber, it was only to wake up in an ever more terrifying nightmare, discovering, every time, that I'd had a limb amputated. The pain never faded, the wound stayed open. I gulped for air. With both feet planted in the dung of my life that seemed to disintegrate like a wafer, I let myself sink.

From the depths of the darkness, I found the strength to push my way back up to the surface. *The show must go on*, as the song goes. As a teenager, I'd sung the line at the top of my lungs. Now, I was living it.

Gradually, a few at a time, I let the people I loved back into my life. With much solicitude, they showered me with worn-out maxims, like prayers mumbled over centuries. I drank in their awkward kindnesses like over-salted chicken soup after a stomach bug. They didn't cure me, but they did save me from myself just a little.

There was no anniversary party celebrated with pomp and circumstance at Hotel Something-Or-Other. No heartfelt speeches about the virtues of promises that endure, no renewed vows, no old aunt with wedding cake in her hair or drunk uncles with wandering hands. And definitely no survivors on the dance floor.

With the money I made from selling my wedding rings, I bought an overpriced pair of stunning blue Italian boots – and I say this without shame, because I wanted my feet to eclipse everything else for a moment. I gave the rest to a youth centre, and they used it to buy a foosball and a ping-pong table. It made me happy to know that somewhere kids were whacking balls around on the scraps of my marriage.

3

In which Claudine tries
unsuccessfully to help me

As people generally tend to do in these situations, my friend and colleague Claudine suggested I focus on the bright side of the breakup. On the silver lining. She'd had the good sense to wait a few months before throwing me a life preserver, knowing – having already been through as much herself – that in the early days rage clouds everything, including the ability to reason.

"Just think, now you won't have to pick up his dirty laundry or wash his nasty underwear."

"I never had to do that anyway."

"Now you have the whole bed to yourself!"

"I hate it. I'm sleeping in the guest room."

"You could sell the house and buy a little condo downtown, nothing to maintain and in walking distance of all the cute cafés."

"But it's the kids' house – they grew up here. They still have their rooms."

"But that's just it, they're not kids anymore."

"Charlotte's coming home for the summer."

"For the summer? *Come on!* Buy a condo with a guest room, that'll do just fine."

"What about when the grandkids come visit?"

"You don't have grandkids!"

"Not yet. But Antoine and his girlfriend are talking about it."

"Antoine? He can barely take care of himself!"

"He's just a little disorganized."

"Buy a condo with an indoor pool. They'll always want to come see you. Then at night they'll get the hell out."

"I'm not ready."

"What about Jacques's family? Didn't you hate his sister, that princess and her little brats?"

"Oh my God, didn't I tell you? I really let her have it!"

"You didn't!"

"Yeah, a few weeks after Jacques left."

• • •

One night, as everyone was talking over each other, Jacques told his sister – who was complaining that she didn't have a life and could never slow down or take time for herself like everyone else – that we could give her a break and take the kids once in a while. I remember feeling my chest tighten as he made the offer. Jacinthe had become a mother, by choice, in her early forties – she'd found the idea of wasting her youth raising kids ridiculous – and now she had two little monsters who didn't understand the meaning of the word "no," had zero respect for people or possessions, got what they wanted when they wanted it, and didn't see the point of being nice. Their undisputed godlike status apparently exempted them from the rules and punishments that would normally fit the crime. Jacinthe didn't need to be told twice: the following Wednesday she showed up with a bag full of supplies for the long evening of babysitting ahead. And for herself: hot yoga, followed by dinner with girlfriends at a trendy bar.

Even though we never repeated the offer, Jacinthe showed up every Wednesday from then on, yoga or not, CrossFit or not. My sweet Jacques, bless him, never could bring himself to tell her that broadly interpreting the expression "every once in a while" for "every single Wednesday" was pushing it. We'd only managed to get out of it the two or three times when I forced Jacques to join me for dinner – at 4:30 in the afternoon. I'd never conceived of pulling such a stunt when my children had been younger, a fact he seemed to overlook when he told me, his eyes full of conviction, "She could use the rest, don't you remember how hard it was with two kids? And George is almost never around." And besides, when darling George was around, he didn't have time to "babysit" his own kids. So I respected Jacques's commitment for nearly two years, mostly because I didn't know how to refuse, but also because I really wanted to break those kids in.

Since she was on the front line when I hurled my Facebook bomb, Jacinthe thought it prudent not to show up that first Wednesday. No doubt her mother had begged her, in the name of the Holy Father who had married me, not to leave the kids with a crazy woman sabotaging family get-togethers. The grandparents never babysat; they were too old to be running after kids and pulling them down from the curtains. The next week, clearly not giving a rat's ass about how I was doing, she showed up at the usual time – just before dinner, of course – with her bag well stocked for the long night ahead.

She jammed her finger furiously against the doorbell several times, her anger melting into a smile once I finally answered.

"Oh, there you are! I was worried you weren't home. Thank God! Boys, stop running! Come here! Auntie Diana's home!!"

"Auntie Diane isn't in the mood to babysit today. I'd probably murder them, with all the patience I have."

"You must be starting to feel better now, no?"

"Not really."

"Well, you seem fine."

"Appearances can be deceiving."

"Okay, I get it. Look, I'll do my class, then just grab an appetizer with the girls and come right back. I won't even go out after."

"Sorry, Jacinthe, I can't today. I'm not up for it. You should have called first."

"I must have called fifty times! You didn't answer!"

"That's because I don't feel like talking or seeing anyone."

"Well, that sucks, it really sucks. I was looking forward to finally having an evening to myself, a little time of my own. Sometimes I wonder how I even stay sane. I spend the whole day running around, and with George never home . . ."

"I know, I get it. Been there, done that. I have three kids, remember? Only I never had an auntie to watch them every week. No one ever offered . . ."

"Well, it's really shitty that my kids have to pay for your breakup. This is the highlight of their week, too."

"Well, go ask your brother! He's still alive, you know!"

She twisted her face into such a scowl, that in that moment she looked just like her mother.

"Right then, I guess I'll have to skip another class. Had I known, I wouldn't have rushed to pick the kids up early. Fantastic! What am I supposed to make for dinner? Okay, boys, we're going! Auntie Diane isn't feeling well!"

"I hope you'll find someone reliable to watch them."

"Someone reliable?"

"I think I've done my part."

"Seriously? You're just going to leave us high and dry? What about the goddamn vacation I have booked! You two break up and life stops, is that it? You tell everyone to go screw themselves and get over it?"

"*My* goddamn vacation is seeing your cheeky ass show up here every week to drop off *your* kids, that your brother offered to watch, not me. Not me! Yet I still babysat them almost *every* week for two years. *Two years!*"

"I don't believe this! All this time, I thought you liked taking care of them!"

"I did, but you know what I'd have liked even better? To watch them *once in a while*, like we'd originally said."

"What's one night a week for you?"

"The same as it is for you! The same exact thing!"

"Your kids are out of the house!"

"And the same goes for your brother! His kids are gone, too. Only I'm all alone and he's got backup!"

"Fine, forget it, we'll just go home. *Fuck* class. So what if I'm on the edge of a nervous breakdown. No big deal. Madame needs all her nights to herself . . ."

"Hey, dipshit! You aren't the one having a hard time, here! I am! *Me!* I'm not pissing anyone off, but you know what? Your brother's pissing me off, you're pissing me off, just about everyone is pissing me off, Christ Almighty! Do what everybody else does and hire a babysitter! Did you ever babysit my kids back when you had all your nights to yourself? No, never. *Never!* Not a single bloody time! What did you do with all your nights alone, you self-centred *bitch*?'

· · ·

"I shouldn't have sworn like that in front of the kids," I said to Claudine, recapping the scene.

"God! I would have *loved* to be there!" she said gleefully.

"Wait, there's more – just before I slammed the door, I heard her mutter something like 'Poor Jacques, now I get it . . .' I almost puked in my mouth."

"What a bitch!"

"So I opened the door and screamed, 'Hey lardass, you've got camel toe! You're too old and fat to wear leggings!'"

"She was wearing leggings as pants?"

"Yup. Patterned ones."

"That must have felt good."

"Not really. I closed the door, then curled up in a ball and cried all night."

"It's nerves."

"I'm really going to miss those little brats."

"Okay, so that's not the bright side. We'll think of something else."

But Claudine's efforts were wasted, and it wasn't helping that Jacques had left. He was the one who took out the trash, the recycling, the compost. He did a lot of the cooking – he was better at it than me – the grocery shopping, paid the bills, remembered important appointments, was never late, always put the toilet seat down, liked wine, good food, my friends, and always brought me home bran nut muffins on Saturday mornings. Other than fewer hairs here and there, I had no reason on the domestic front to be glad he was gone. "Someone Else" was probably in the process of discovering that her lover was also a kind companion who was good at multitasking. She would never let him get away. That's the problem when you've done too good a job choosing your husband: afterwards it's tough to have to share him.

"But you must have been so sick of hearing the same stories for the past twenty-five years."

"No, he was good at telling them."

"Then he was a bad dresser."

"No."

"Did he snore?"

"No."

"Stink?"

"No."

"Not even when he exercised?"

"Not even."

"Was he disorganized?"

"Not compared to me."

"Maybe he didn't listen to you, or he just feigned interest?"

"No."

"He spent Saturday mornings washing the car in front of the garage."

"He never washed the car."

"He wore socks with sandals."

"No."

"And he was always patient?"

"Like he had all the time in the world."

Once we'd finished going through it all, I felt like I was dangling above a bottomless pit. Each of his non-faults exposed a little more of my own, all of which left me with the distinct impression that I had never been, in all our years together, good enough for the man who probably had married me more out of goodwill than love.

"Stop, you're being ridiculous. Now you're in the stage where you think your ex is some kind of god and you're shit in comparison. It's normal, don't let it get to you – it'll pass. He couldn't have been *that* great, you'll see that when you get to the 'letting go' stage. We'll find something else in the meantime."

"There's no point."

"It'll help pass the time. Because it really will take time, lots of time. And as it doesn't look like he's going to turn into an asshole any time soon –"

"He'll never be an asshole."

"– we might have to resort to drastic measures."

"Like?"

"There's an almost sure-fire way to flip things around."

"*Pfff . . .*"

"But I know it's not your kind of thing. I do know lots of people who've done it, but you may not like the idea, and I respect that. I'm not sure it would be all that helpful anyway . . ."

"You're being really cryptic."

"Maybe Jacques was more than just a nice husband, darling."

"No. He's human, everybody is, but he was always a perfect gentleman with me."

"What a stupid thing to say! He cheated on you. He played you! And he called you boring to your face!"

I used to believe that if we say them often enough, words become worn and faded, little slivers of soap that slip between your fingers – but I was wrong. They had taken on a terrible destructive force, covering me like a slick of oil. *Boring.* It sliced through me like a dagger.

"That was a real cheap shot. You're just a . . ."

"A what? Come on! A *what?* Get angry! At me if you have to! I can take it! Hate me – hate anyone! Jacques isn't coming back. It's over, honey. He left you for a thirty-year-old bombshell!"

"You're only saying that because you're bitter Philippe never came back."

"Well, Jacques isn't coming back either. You're in denial, honey. Move on, it's been months! He's a prick like all the rest. He wanted some fresh ass, like they all do."

"It's a phase, a rough patch. It's just a fling –"

"No! He moved in with her! Earth to Diane! He's gone. Wake up!"

"But . . . we're married . . ."

She took a step back, as though I'd just told her I had Ebola.

"Okay. Let's get one thing clear. You need to stop saying that. Everyone keeps laughing at you during lunch."

"Stop saying what?"

"When you talk about the breakup, you always bring up how you're married."

"But being married means something."

"No, Diane, it doesn't mean a thing. When the love runs out, it runs out. Married or not. It's not some magic spell, marriage – a ring doesn't protect you from anything."

"But marriage makes relationships stronger, they last longer. There are statistics to prove it!"

"But the statistics don't say anything about love."

"You're cynical, and that's sad."

"Well, you're out of touch, Diane. And that's pathetic."

Lucky for me, when you're a mum in an age where the technology that pulls the strings of our lives changes with the seasons, you get called "out of touch" every single day, both literally and figuratively. A knife slicing through soft butter. It's no big deal.

I dragged my boring, out-of-touch woman's carcass over to the restaurant where Charlotte was waiting for me. Charlotte, my sweet, soon-to-be veterinarian of a daughter, almost too smart to be my offspring, had been checking in on me even more frequently since her father left. Tender and devoted, my daughter would save the whole world if she could. In fact, I suspect she wanted to be a veterinarian because animals are easier to handle. With just a little love and care, animals offer themselves up like the gullible to a guru – the difference being the only thing you get in return is affection.

Contrary to habit, when the server galloped over to take my order, I asked for a big glass of white wine. I needed to re-centre myself so I could play the mum keeping her head above water.

"Hi, Mum!"

"Hi, sweetie! How did your exams go?"

"Uh . . . the term hasn't started."

"Oh, right. Sorry. I'm a bit out of it. So, how are things?"

"Great."

"Have you spoken to your father?"

"Yes."

"When?"

"Day before yesterday, I think."

"How's he doing?"

"Good, good."

"I'm glad."

I'd devised an agenda that I followed to the letter whenever I saw the kids: I'd ask about school or work, Jacques, their love life, upcoming projects. This way, I don't forget anything and give the impression that we can discuss anything, even him, without it being awkward. The first few times I'd even written the list on my hand.

"I stopped by the house before coming over. I see you demolished your bed frame."

"I had to break it into pieces to fit it through the door."

"We could have taken it apart."

"Bah. It would have been too complicated. The sledgehammer did the job."

"Did you buy another one?"

"Not yet."

Somewhere in a tiny compartment at the back of my brain, the notion that I should wait to ask Jacques before choosing a new one germinated.

"What was the rush to get rid of it?"

I stayed quiet, avoiding her question.

"I thought maybe we could go shopping?"

"Do you need something?"

"No, Mum, just to look around. Whenever's good for you."

"Okay."

"It's always fun to buy something new when you're feeling down, right?"

"You're feeling down?"

"Mum . . ."

"Hey, I've got an idea. Why don't I take the afternoon off? Are you free?"

• • •

The girl selling me jeans was wearing her own much too tight. Though she must have started with two cheeks, now there was only one, divided by a seam that struggled to contain her considerable flab. I was observing, not judging.

She wanted me to try on a bunch of skinny jeans, made out of some kind of stretchy fabric similar to leggings that barely hides the contours of a woman's crotch and does absolutely nothing for her figure. Charlotte, who was standing behind the salesgirl, mimed a big "time out" each time she disapproved. My ideal pair was still the sexy comfort promised by Levis ads of the eighties. I was a little out of touch for sure.

In the fitting-room mirror, under the cruel fluorescence of neon lighting, my gaze unusually clarified by the two glasses of white from lunch, I beheld my body in all its disgrace. Despite the weight I'd lost in the past few weeks, my legs appeared heavy, soft and ill-suited to support a body. My wrinkled shirt crept up over the equally soft bulge of my belly. My breasts, too small to make an impression or be described as voluptuous, wisely stayed under the fabric. Every part of me said *boring*: my chubby limbs, my thin, limp hair, my eyes ringed with dark circles, my beige clothing, and the natural tones of my complexion. No wonder a man like Jacques ended up tired of me; lassitude had carved a niche into every cell of my being.

I crumpled to the floor, lying on the grime of all those who had been there before me. I couldn't get up, couldn't talk. Pain nailed me to the ground, as if gravity had suddenly tripled in force. From under the door I could see the feet of people going about their everyday lives, and I envied them. If I couldn't stand out in life, maybe I could stand out in death: I'd never heard of someone struck down by the weight of their ugliness, their lifeless body discovered inside a fitting room.

Once Charlotte realized I wasn't coming out or answering her, she slid underneath the door to find me, crawling on her hands and knees so she wouldn't scrape her spine. She curled up next to me and took me into her big, I'm-all-grown-up arms without saying a word. My Charlotte. My baby. In her silence I could hear the "It'll be okay, Mum," and "I love you, Mum." She was hardly breathing, as if she, too, wanted to disappear. She had dived alongside me into the quicksand, demanding nothing. It made me want to dig in my heels and resist going under.

"How're you doing on sizes in there?" came the voice of the saleswoman.

"Great!"

"What do you think of the skinny jeans?"

"They're great, too!"

And just as quickly as I had been levelled, I started to laugh like a madwoman. My whole body shook. And the more I tried to hold back my laughter, the harder I laughed. It was contagious. Charlotte started to laugh too. It was beautiful. Two women on their knees, one half-naked, clutching each other on the dirty fitting-room floor, tears streaming down their faces. Truly, beautiful.

"Remember how, when you were little, you'd always accidentally lock yourself in public washrooms?"

"Yes!"

"Every time I'd tell you not to lock the door, but you'd do it anyway!"

"I know. And I could never unlock it afterwards. I'm not sure why. I think I would just panic."

"So I would crawl underneath the stall."

"One time there wasn't enough room underneath, so you went over top."

"Really?"

"At the Château Laurier. You were wearing a dress, and you weren't too happy."

"Oh my gosh – yeah, I remember."

We emerged fifteen minutes later, faces stained with dried tears, still shaking with laughter from all the memories that had come flooding back. The salesgirl kept such a straight face we were convinced the entire chain had banned smiling completely. But I got it; there was nothing to laugh about when jeans made by the hands of exploited Bangladeshi workers cost nearly $200 a pair simply to make a pack of bourgeoisie with a sick conscience feel chic. And nothing to laugh about when, claiming I didn't have a choice, I bought them.

• • •

When she noticed I hadn't come back to work after lunch, Claudine texted me a few times. She absolutely *had* to tell me something very important and wanted me to call her back.

"I'm sorry," she said.

"Me too."

"But I just wanted to tell you something that might help."

"No, you wanted to tell me how to start thinking of Jacques as an asshole."

"No, no, that's not it."

"Can you just tell me?"

"Never mind, it's a bad idea."

"I want to know. *Shoot*."

"You sure?"

"Yes."

"Private investigator."

"Private investigator? What do you think a P.I. could possibly tell me? That my husband ran off with a tramp?"

"That's what I said, it's not a good idea."

"But you thought it might help anyway."

"Yeah. Because sometimes when we could really use a pick-me-up, it's nice to find out that things didn't always go the way we think they did."

"What does that mean?"

"*Arrrgh* . . . I should've kept my mouth shut."

"Well, you didn't, so out with it!"

"You think Jacques is a saint, but I doubt he is."

"Why wouldn't he be?"

"Statistics aren't in his favour."

"Who cares about statistics?"

"Well . . ."

"Spit it out, Claudine!"

"How long was he dating Charlene before he left you?"

"Jacques and I must have gone over it about ten times, and I bet I told you just as many times."

"He told you what he wanted you to hear."

"But he left me for her! How does that change anything now?"

"What if he was seeing her for two years before he left you?"

"Oh, come on – it was a new thing! Or relatively new. Charlene had only been at the office six months when he left."

"Okay. But even if it was new with her, which would surprise me, but okay, what if before her . . ."

"What?"

"Do you think it's the first time he's done something like this?"

I didn't answer.

"An investigator won't change the past. It's just to turn things around, and for you to stop thinking he's such a saint."

I kept quiet.

"Diane?"

I was turning her words over.

"Diane?"

"I'm thinking."

"No, don't. There's no point. Drop it. Just forget it."

"You know something I don't."

"No, I swear. It's just that the whole story is so cliché! It's just to see if Jacques, just overnight . . . you know, I never managed a final count of all the students Philippe slept with?"

"I feel like such an idiot."

"No, don't! Just forget it."

"I guess you have a name for me? Someone you'd recommend?"

"Do you want the good news now? It's actually a great idea – and why I really called. It's not about something you lost, but about something you never had. Something you might be able to do now!"

"Hmm . . ."

"Something you could never do with Jacques."

"I don't know what that could be, apart from sleeping with other guys."

"You're forgetting something important. You used to talk to me about it all the time . . ."

"I'm stumped."

"No idea?

"Come on, Claudine."

"That's what Cloclo is here for!"

"Okay, lady, fill me in."

"You'll finally be able to . . . French kiss!"

"Seriously? *That's* what this is about? I couldn't care less about making out!"

"Oh come on! Tongue! *TONGUE!* It's been, what, twenty-five years? How many times did you tell me you missed doing it, you dreamed of it, but that Jacques never liked it with tongue?"

"But that's not a life goal!"

"I'm not giving you a life goal. I'm giving you a good reason to get your ass in gear! You're smart, you're pretty . . ."

"Don't even try. I just went shopping."

"No one looks good in a fitting room."

"I'm squishy."

"That won't matter for kissing! Wear some compression tights until you get back in shape and everything will be hunky-dory!"

"*Pfff* . . ."

"You're beautiful, Diane, don't doubt it. You're so damn beautiful. I'd hate you if I didn't like you so much."

"Don't overdo it."

"Name one guy you'd French kiss. Quick! Without thinking!"

"This is silly. I feel like I'm fourteen."

"You're not far off, if we take away the twenty-five years you spent with Jacques."

"Twenty-eight: we'd been together for three years before we got married."

"Even worse! You've got to start somewhere! The French kiss is kind of like the one-metre diving board. You've got to practise on the lower one before you move up to ten metres."

"Weird analogy."

"I know. Come on, give me a name."

"I don't feel like making out with anyone."

"A name!"

"J.P.!"

"You mean fourth-floor J.P.? In Accounting?"

"Yeah, why?"

"I don't know, maybe you're aiming too high. And I think he's married. I'll have to check."

"You asked me for a name!"

"Of course, that's great! Excellent! We'll go with J.P. since he was the first one you came up with. Focus on him. And anyway, we're only talking about French kissing."

"Oh right, real easy."

"Easier than you think, Diane. Much easier."

"It worries me a bit that you say that."

"If you only knew how right I am."

"I want the name of your detective."

"I've got a good shrink, too."

. . .

Charlotte was snuggled into her big fluffy blanket watching an episode of an American series that I just "had to see" on her computer. She must have said as much thirty times over the past couple of years. But I'd been so far behind since *Six Feet Under* that I gave up trying. Like I said, out of touch.

"So, do you regret buying the jeans?"

"No way, kiddo. I love them. If you say they look good on me, I'll believe you."

"Well, it's true!"

"Uh-huh."

"You're a knockout for your age, I'm telling you."

"For my age."

"You're a knockout, period."

"Uh-huh."

"I swear."

"Have you been talking to Claudine?"

"Claudine? No. Why?"

"You sound like her."

"That's because you're beautiful. Everyone thinks so."

"Yeah . . ."

"Not yeah. Yes."

"Thanks, honey. You're sweet. So, what do you think of Nautilus?"

"Ugh. It costs an arm and a leg, and everyone who goes there thinks they're so hot. You want to do bicep curls?"

"Well, I should probably start doing something. It can't hurt."

"What about jogging? You can jog anywhere, plus it's free. And it's really trendy."

I hate trendy.

4

In which I gauge the cost of words

"**H**OW DO YOU FEEL?"

Claudine had reminded me over and over again before my first appointment: "You've got to be open, ready to bare it all, to face things head on. You can swear, you can cry, you can throw yourself on the ground and scream, but you've got to talk, you understand? It'll be tough, you'll feel like you're going in circles, but that's normal. The closer you get to the real knot, the tougher it'll be. This lady, she'll help you, but only if you help yourself. You've got to help yourself. She's not a cleaning woman, it's not her job to polish your insides and make your ego shine. You're going to face all your demons and it's going to hurt."

I was supercharged when I arrived, ready to unpack all the vicissitudes of my soul on the couch of a perfect stranger, recipient of innumerable diplomas. I was so electrified that not even her resemblance to the disgraced Jian Ghomeshi's lawyer could bring me down.

"Like shit."

"What a picture."

"It's the first word that came to me."

"Why do you think that is?"

"Because that's how I feel."

"Do you feel like that often, Mrs. Delaunais?"

"Please, call me Diane."

It's a nicety we get used to saying as we grow older, the occasions multiplying with alarming frequency. People have been addressing me by my last name for so long that I jump every time the cashier at the grocery store calls me "Diane" when she asks if I need a bag. I'd be completely grey by now if I didn't dye my hair. The colour changed so quickly I could have given Marie Antoinette a run for her money.

"Do you often use that expression to describe how you're feeling?"

"No."

"Only since the separation?"

"I think so, yes."

"Why is that?"

The first knot. Like trying to swallow soda crackers without water.

"Because my husband doesn't love me anymore."

"Does that make you feel less of a good person now?"

"Maybe . . . yeah."

"What has changed, do you think?"

"Oh, lots of things."

"Like what?"

"Well . . . I feel ugly."

"In what sense?"

"In every sense."

"Physically?"

"And in other ways."

"Can you expand on that?"

"It's hard to put it into words."

"What do you see when you look in the mirror?" To be sure I was getting my money's worth, I'd discreetly started the timer on my wristwatch and had promised myself I'd talk fast and answer quickly. We hadn't even passed the seven-minute mark and already the words had slowed in my throat, like larva slowly crawling their way out. I had come in, certain I wouldn't lose it; the session probably wouldn't go as planned.

"Skin. Saggy, pale skin."

"Is that new?"

"No! Of course not . . ."

"So what's different now?"

"I can see myself better."

"Better?"

"I can see all the details I glossed over before, the stuff that didn't used to bother me. With age I've thickened everywhere, lost the spring in my step, my stomach is flabby, streaked with stretch marks, and my that's-it flaps everywhere . . ."

"Your what?"

"My 'that's-it' – the skin that jiggles when you raise your arm to say, 'That's it!'"

The therapist raised her arm and flexed it, curious to see how gravity was affecting her own triceps. It was tactless of her; she knew full well nothing would jiggle.

"And before, you accepted yourself the way you were?"

"I think so. At least, I thought it was normal to put on a bit of weight, for my body to change like everyone else's."

"But you don't think so now?"

"No."

"And why is that?"

"I just realized I've kind of dropped the ball."

"How so?"

"I've let myself go."

"Do you think it has anything to do with the fact that Jacques left you for a younger woman?"

"A much younger woman."

"Yes, much younger."

"Well . . . maybe."

"If Jacques had left you for a woman in her fifties who had your 'flaws' – let's just call them that for the moment – would you be this hard on yourself?"

I was only forty-eight. Rounding me up to the next decade robbed me of two precious years I wasn't about to give up without a fight. Diplomacy, definitely not her strong suit.

"I think that would have been even worse."

"Really? Why is that?"

"Because the problem would've been me – me as a person."

"But in this case . . ."

"It might just be about sex."

"Did you and Jacques ever talk about it?"

"About what?"

"The reasons he decided to leave."

"Yes, of course."

"And?"

"It's complicated . . ."

"Was he not satisfied, sexually?"

"No, I don't think that was it. But you don't have to be a rocket scientist to see why a guy his age is with a thirty-year-old."

"What were his reasons?"

"I don't know why we're talking about him. I came to talk about me."

"We're trying to see what's gotten twisted in your own mirror."

Had the silence that followed not been costing me so much, I'd have let it go on longer. Much longer. Second knot, thirteenth minute. A knot sinking down my throat.

"He told me that . . . that he . . ."

"Uh-huh."

I had to cut the sentence into pieces so I could get it out.

"He told you he . . ."

"Wanted . . ."

"Uh-huh . . ."

"To be . . ."

"He told you he wanted to be . . ."

She was searching my eyes, waiting for the abscess to drain. It had formed somewhere in my soul and was threatening to infect it irredeemably. This woman knew it; she didn't believe the story was just about sex.

"Happy."

Jacques wanted to be happy.

Jacques was no longer happy with me.

Jacques could be happy with Her.

Jacques wanted to be with her.

Goddamn fucking logic.

I spent the rest of the session crying like a baby, face buried in my hands. The gentle doctor, a true professional, patiently handed me a few tissues with aloe. I walked out with a blotchy face, but a well-moisturized nose.

5

In which I reveal my sixth toe

I WAS BORN BORING. The gene in question slipped into the double helix of my DNA during conception. I can't dance; it's impossible for me to follow any sort of beat. And it's not about my hearing – my parents took me to a handful of specialists when I was young. My brain's the culprit: it can detect sounds but can't coordinate the movements to go with them. Unlike the rhythmically gifted, I am condemned to guesswork. Every time I move my feet, it's to catch up to the tempo. I manage to keep the beat only by accident, and very rarely at that. I'm officially rhythmically challenged, which is unfortunately a disability you can't see. I'd have preferred a sixth toe; at least then surgery is an option.

It wasn't a big deal when I was younger. I blended in with the mass of kids waving their arms every which way. My moves on the dance floor really astonished the crowd. People held their stomachs or covered their mouths as they laughed, my mum clapped to the beat to encourage me, and everyone was happy. Especially me. I always gave it my all, and life gave it right back. I miss that innocence.

Things took a turn for the worse when my mother, seeing my shortcomings as a sure sign of artistic talent, signed me up for Introduction to Ballet/Jazz at the renowned Lapierre School of Dance. But, after several weeks of overt exasperation that baffled me entirely, the instructor told my mother I was a lost cause. That was the first time I heard the expression "rhythmically challenged." My mother replied that at any rate, it was a heck of a price tag to teach kids how to "monkey about like any five-year-old could do on her own." There were times I really loved my mother.

In my friends' basements, on the threshold of adolescence, I was assigned special roles, ones that generally didn't require any movement and served mainly to support the other girls' choreography; I spotted their pirouettes, was a pole for their arabesques, a base for the pyramids and even, when necessary, a brace for ones who needed help with their handstands. I'd have been treated no differently if I'd had only one leg. My friends had big hearts; they were protecting me from ridicule.

Once we started going to church basement parties, I developed a knack for seeming as if I were constantly on the dance floor, though I wasn't: I went from friend to friend, whispering secrets in their ears. I followed them to the bathroom, the snack bar, and even outside when some wanted to sneak a cigarette. When the dance floor was so packed there was hardly any space at all, I'd venture a few movements that were rapidly engulfed in the chaos of limbs knocking together. The rest of the time, I went around like everyone else, calling people "losers" or "fat cows" or "pizza face." Suffering from acne or being rhythmically challenged, it was all the same struggle.

Some of the best moments of my life were during the U2 craze. Dancing to them was easy, all you had to do was keep your feet stuck together and sway your body like seaweed in a gentle current with your eyes closed, arms undulating in the air. The general fluidity completely concealed my lack of rhythm. Some nights, U2 was the only band we played. It was nirvana, and we ended up in an almost trance-like state. Even today, I get a rush when I hear those first few notes of "Sunday Bloody Sunday." Sundays are still tinged with the memories.

In university, cheap beer and the time we'd spend waiting in line for it gave me lots of easy outs. I became the self-proclaimed Queen of Refills and spent most nights doing runs between the bar and our "spot" (usually a pile of purses in a corner). I knew the servers, my friends, the DJs. The finest music flowed like water through our intoxicated bodies and electrified minds. And there, in rapture over the new bottle opener some mechanical engineering students had devised, is where I met Jacques. Like me, he was taken with a tool the bartender was using to open six beer bottles at a time – while they were still in the case. A stroke of genius to slake our thirst. Those guys knew how to prioritize. I'd just ordered five beers and he'd ordered six, but he offered to help me carry them nonetheless.

"You've already got six!"

"I can carry ten."

"Ten?"

"One per finger. Like this."

He'd plunged his fingers into the plastic cups, poking them through the heads of foam undisturbed by whatever filth had collected on his hands since he'd last washed them. I pictured the sweat, hair grease, snot, and germs from money, keys, handshakes . . .

"This way I won't drop them."

"Makes sense."

"Are you alone?"

"No, with friends."

"Where?"

"We're at the back, over there."

I'd pointed to the far end of the room, past the mass of bodies bouncing to the beat of the *"Jump! Jump! Jump!"* blasting through speakers that wouldn't last the night. Jacques had revealed a set of beautiful straight, white teeth. A guy with a good upbringing.

"I've got an idea," he said.

"What?"

"Let's drop them off and meet outside at door B."

"For a smoke?"

"To get some air."

"You don't want to dance?"

"Nah, I suck."

This frank declaration, so seemingly anodyne, would determine the rest of my life. Jacques, like me, was rhythmically challenged. Watching him move however he wanted, wonderfully defying the beat of the song, made me feel like the shipwrecked do when they first glimpse signs of civilization. I fell in love with the guy for what he didn't have. All his endearing qualities came to life for a moment in the shadow of this absence, which made me treasure them all the more. Had I been religious, I might have believed God had sent Jacques to apologize for overlooking me when bestowing a sense of rhythm on the world.

We spent that first night, like everyone swept up in love, entangled in passionate embraces, drinking in the same air, trying to fuse our bodies into one. If he had told me then that he didn't like French kissing, I wouldn't have believed him. But it later crossed my mind that such kisses, like women's eggs, were numbered; once the well ran dry, you had to learn to go without. Nights just slipped away. I wouldn't feel that exhausted again until I had children. We loved each other like no one else, obviously. And just like everyone else, our marriage was for *forever*.

In mathematics, two negatives make a positive; in biology, it's not so simple. When Alexandre was born, I'd deployed an arsenal of means to make sure my son's brain fired the necessary synapses and neuromuscular junctions for him to keep a beat. I bought a metronome to teach him to clap his hands in sync, as well as DVDs of nursery rhymes, songs, and dances so his ears would be constantly stimulated. When he was eighteen months, I enrolled him in a parent-baby music class that promised to "awaken every child's inner music." I endured a whole half-dozen humiliating sessions before giving up on the class and going back to DVDs in order to stimulate the hormone in question. The "therapist" had decided I wouldn't leave her workshops without "taming the cacophony" inside me – I'll spare you the psychobabble on which she based her approach. It wasn't the first time someone had tried to fix me, but her method verged on assault: she would grab my shoulders and force me to move with her, or clap her hands close to my ears so that my body would "wake up." I left before I hit her.

By four, Alexandre was old enough to take ballet – the only class without parental participation. It didn't take long to realize he'd been spared, his body evidently able to comply with even the most demanding cadences.

When he came out at fourteen, my mother-in-law didn't waste any time offering up a simplistic explanation, one of her specialties. "You can't be surprised, what with all those dance classes you made him take." I still don't know how I managed to contain myself. Over the next few days I quelled my rage by imagining myself gouging out her eyes, breaking her nose, or kicking her stomach so hard I crushed her intestines. Violent? Not nearly as violent as thinking homosexuality is a defect.

Charlotte and Antoine can also keep a beat. I have a lot of respect for mathematical laws.

6

In which Jean-Paul becomes my rebound

CLAUDINE'S CHILDISH SUGGESTIONS EVENTUALLY metamorphosed into a sort of role-playing game that kept my mind off things. Her plan had worked. I'd even hatched a series of terrifically corny storylines fit for the most ridiculous soap operas, all ending with a kiss from J.P.:

1. By pure coincidence, I end up in the copy room, face to face with Jean-Paul. He doesn't object when I close the door and lean in for a kiss.
2. The elevator breaks down – we're the only two inside, obviously – and he comes over to see if I am okay and ends up gathering me into his arms for a kiss that I don't resist in the slightest.
3. I'm taking the stairs to get in a little exercise before sitting down at my desk for the day, and we run into each other – he's working out at the same time, what a coincidence! – and this inevitably leads to an impromptu make-out session.
4. Etc.

My bank of storylines also include a few catastrophes that just about bring me to tears:

1. A bomb threat forces us to leave the building, and in the panic of the evacuation we wind up alone together a few streets over. We cling to each other, lips locked in an effort to fend off the evil surrounding us.
2. A classic power outage: darkness, fear, beads of sweat, fortunate coincidences, a tangle of hands and mouths, in that order or rather, disorder.
3. I faint in the hallway outside the conference room and J.P., in a burst of Olympian heroism, catches me just before my head hits the concrete of our LEED-certified building (averting damage to my brain and a messy clean-up). He's so relieved when I come to that he can't help leaning in for a hungry kiss.
4. Etc.

On other occasions, I pushed the drama to ridiculous heights, the details of which you'll forgive me for not sharing here. In the best of these worst-case scenarios, we are the only survivors of an apocalypse and only a kiss can distract us from the harrowing wait for our inevitable end. In brief, things look bad, but at least we're making out.

In the real world, J.P. worked in Finance on the fourth floor and I was in Physical Resources, one floor up. The chances of winding up alone in an elevator, or in a burning wood nearby, were next to zero. I'd have to help things along a bit.

So I multiplied my trips between the lobby and the fifth floor to increase my chances of running into him, statistically speaking. I had to start somewhere. I had to get to that rebound. I took the stairs down and the elevator up – I couldn't ruin things by sweating – telling people all the exercise during breaks and over lunch was part of a new health kick. Given my situation, everyone understood my need to shake things up. I did routine checks of the fourth floor much more than was necessary (to be honest, I was just pretending to blow my nose in the bathroom), or I might forget this or that to give myself a few more opportunities to test my chances that were, I was forced to admit, far better in my dreams than in real life.

When, in the elevator, I did end up with J.P. (and a whole bunch of chaperones), I focused on him intensely and tried telepathy: they say such messages reach the target more easily when you're both in the same room. So I'd look straight at him and order him, very simply and clearly, to kiss me. But he didn't hear me. People walked in and out of the elevator, nodding politely before turning to watch the floor indicators light up. The longer I stared, the more beautiful I found him – and the more unlikely it seemed we would ever lock lips.

"Don't be ridiculous!' said Claudine. 'This isn't voodoo – you've got to actually *do* something. Go see him, buy him coffee. You'll never kiss him if you don't make a move. Telepathy, hah! If you say you got that from *The Secret*, I'll kill you."

"It was in a magazine."

"Don't tell me which one. Come by later, I need you to run an errand for me."

Foolishly, I walked back to Claudine's office after my break. "Oh, Diane!" she said, loud enough for everyone to hear. "Are you going down to Accounting? Could you give this to J.P. for me?"

After taking the couple of files she'd retrieved from the archives, I went down a floor and walked resolutely over to Jean-Paul's office. The door was open, so I went in. Piles of neatly stacked folders waited for attentive hands beside a fake crystal glass full of Pilot Hi-Tecpoint V7 Grip pencils (I made a slight grimace – I hate medium tips). A few inches away, a little porcelain shepherd smiled at me, looking after his imaginary sheep as if there weren't wolves to worry about. No photographs, just a peace lily that seemed happy to be there. Which doesn't mean a thing, of course; peace lilies are happy anywhere. J.P.'s secretary rushed over to greet me.

"Hello, Diane!"

"Oh, hi, Josy!"

"Are you looking for Jean-Paul?"

Nobody called him Jean-Paul except his secretary. A question of pecking order, I suppose. He always introduced himself as J.P, what with the stock of "Jean-Paul" having plummeted since a popular soap opera had featured a villain by that name.

"Uh . . . yes, I am."

"Are those files for him?"

"Uh, no – well, yes. Claudine asked me to deliver them, but I'd rather hand them to him in person."

"Don't worry, I'll see that he gets them. He should be back soon."

"Where is he?"

"He went for a coffee on the second floor. They just bought an espresso machine."

"Oh, *wow!*"

"The translation department has special coffee needs."

"I'll go down and find him,' I said. 'There are a few things I should explain anyway."

"I like your outfit."

"Oh, thanks!"

If I'd been blind, I might have returned the compliment. But as I watched her head back to her office on her glossy white four-inch stiletto heels, I felt a sort of pity.

She waved at me, fluttering her white acrylic nails and white pearl rings perfectly accessorizing the white earrings, bracelets, decorative comb, and eye shadow that matched her pantsuit. She'd gained a reputation as a busybody from the moment she'd arrived and lived up to it on every occasion. If I had a secretary like that, I'd probably spend breaks exploring the building until I found an espresso machine on a faraway floor, too.

I took the stairs, giving myself time to muster up some courage. When I reached the second floor, I saw J.P. slip into the elevator with the energetic stride of a man splendidly in shape. I hurried to catch him, but the door closed at the very moment I squeaked out a "Jaaaay-Peeee!" That's exactly how it sounded, my greeting ridiculously stretched out. I stood there, bogus files in hand. Almost immediately, the door reopened, revealing a smiling and clearly curious J.P.

"Ah . . . uh. Here, Claudine asked me to give you these, since I was heading to the fourth floor anyway . . ."

"They must be important if you came all the way down here."

"No, no, I'm here for the coffee machine."

"What are they, those files?"

"Uh . . . no idea."

"Oh, okay . . . I think I already approved those last week . . ."

"Maybe she was confused."

"Maybe. Odd, though. Are you going up?"

"Umm . . . yeah."

"But didn't you want a coffee?"

"Oh right, silly me. I forgot."

"All right, then. Well, thanks for the files, I'll look over them right away. There must be something wrong with them."

"Yeah . . ."

"Bye!"

"Uh . . ."

A quiet *whoosh* as the doors closed on silly me. I abandoned the idea of coffee and climbed the stairs at a gentle trot, hoping to digest my disappointment in peace.

I walked into Claudine's office and flopped into the grievances chair. It's the most popular chair in the building.

"I'm done with this whole kissing business. I looked like an idiot, I hate myself, and frankly, J.P. is –"

"– an excellent rebound."

"No, he's way too hot."

"He's independent, a little big-headed, though he can't possibly be as confident as he seems. He's the ideal candidate for you!"

"And he has a wife – or better yet, a girlfriend!"

"What do you care? It's perfect. We're not talking marriage, we're not even talking sex. You just want a little tongue action. Then you can both get on with your lives."

"You want me to get back at Jacques?"

"Not at all. It's not about revenge, it's about putting yourself first. Now's the time to focus on you – and you need two things: to pass the time, and gain a bit of self-confidence back."

"Well, that really worked!"

"How long have you been fantasizing about J.P.?"

"It's not like that."

"Don't tell me it didn't take your mind off things."

"Barely."

"And don't tell me you're not trying a little harder when you get dressed in the morning."

"Maybe a little."

"There you go. That's what the make-out fantasy is all about. As harmless as hot water and lemon, and just as good for you. I haven't seen you look this good in months."

I returned to my desk to find a message from Jean-Paul Boisvert on my answering machine. I couldn't believe it: J.P. had called *me*. The Tom Brady of Accounting had dialled *my* extension.

". . . listen, Diane, uh . . . if you could come by my office when you get a chance. It's nothing important. When you have a minute."

"Just like that?"

"Yup."

"Hey now! Miss I-looked-like-an-idiot . . ."

"Well, what do I do?"

"I imagine that's a rhetorical question."

"But I'll look like an idiot!"

"You will, but you're still going down there."

"Keep the grievances chair warm for me. I'll be right back."

The door to his office was closed – a defence against the threat of unsolicited bedazzlement. Josy, after announcing me over the phone, opened the door like an overzealous butler, with a swish of the arm out of *The Price is Right*. J.P. was concentrating on his computer screen, his brow furrowed and more gorgeous than ever. Worry looked good on him – it gave him a touch of wisdom male models lacked. His hair was so thick I doubted anyone could run a hand through it – not even a slender woman's hand. As for Jacques, his hair had steadily jumped ship until there was nothing but a monk's crown around his head. But since men look sexier with wrinkles, a clean shave was enough to take a good ten years off him; he was one of those older men who wear baldness well. Sometimes I'd felt as if I was the victim of a pernicious shift in our lousy marriage. I took on double the years as time passed – mine, and his.

"Oh! Hello, Diane! Thank you, Josy. You can close the door on your way out."

"Do you want me to take your calls so you won't be disturbed?"

"No, no, you can send them through. Not a problem."

"Ah! This is an informal meeting?"

"No, it's a professional one. Thank you, Josy."

Once the door was closed, J.P. rolled his chair around the desk and next to me, then spoke to me in a hushed, confidential tone. "Listen, Diane, I'm a little uncomfortable asking you this – even a little embarrassed – but I couldn't help noticing earlier . . ."

I didn't hear the rest. I could see his mouth was moving, his hands gesticulating, but for long seconds, what he said completely escaped me. Radio silence. I was hypnotized by his beautiful hands, his perfect mouth. Which was all I needed. That he might employ them to other ends than kissing me bothered me not one bit. When his lips stopped moving, he placed his hands gently on the desk and widened his eyes to indicate it was my turn to speak.

"Uh . . ."

"I'm sorry, it was rude of me to ask."

"No! No, no . . . uh . . . I just didn't hear. I didn't hear what you said."

"Oh?"

"I zoned out. I'm sorry."

Like I said, I looked like an idiot.

"Okay. Uh . . . I asked where you bought your boots. I like them, and my wife's birthday is coming up . . ."

"You're married?"

"Yes."

"Oh, that's funny. I didn't think you were. It's rare, for your generation."

"Uh . . . I think we're . . . about the same age."

"Oh really? How old are you?"

"Forty-four."

"No way!"

"Yes way."

"Impossible."

"Very possible."

"You can't be!"

He didn't look a day past thirty-five. I could have slapped him and his adorable crow's feet. Behind him, through the poorly washed bay window I could make out a corner of the Plains of Abraham, their historic beauty trampled by a motley group of creatures come to re-enact some bucolic scene before returning to their concrete cages. I imagined throwing myself out of the window and, without so much as a blink, could almost feel the grass under my feet. Suddenly, I felt the urge to run.

"What size shoe does she wear?"

"Eight."

"Perfect."

I got up and, leaning against the corner of his desk for balance, took off my boots and placed them on top of the neat stack of files waiting for him. He tried hard to stop me – to convince me to put them back on – but I assured him they were new, that he wouldn't find any others like them, and that they hurt anyway.

"No, really, it's so generous of you, but I don't want *your* boots, I just wanted to know where you bought them. Don't be ridiculous, I can't take the shoes off your feet. Come on, Diane, please, you can't leave like that."

"It's okay. You made me realize I'd rather people looked at my eyes, not my feet."

"Okay, I offended you, I'm sorry. Your boots are beautiful, it's just . . ."

I turned around, opened the door – no Josy, thank God! – and took off in socks down the corridors of the fourth floor, onto the ice-cold concrete of the stairwell, to the fifth floor. I ran, arms pumping, like Wonder Woman. I shot out of there, like I used to do in grade school at the sound of the bell. It felt great: everything seemed lighter, less bureaucratic, less stifling. Whenever I passed someone along the way, I made the sign of the devil's horns to indicate there was nothing to worry about, that it was just a fleeting moment of madness. They could all go back to their paperwork, to the insufferable boredom of it all, but me, I had to run. And oh, how I ran! In my head, I was Lola, Forrest, Alexis the Trotter. I stopped when I reached the closed conference room door, lungs heaving, dark stains of sweat under my arms, socks blackened with dirt.

And that's how Claudine found me, a complete mess. I smiled at her, flashing teeth yellowed from years of drinking coffee and red wine. I was fine, obviously.

"You should try this one day, it's fantastic!"

And then I ran back into the stairwell, laughing like a girl without boots, without reason, without a husband.

I asked the taxi driver to take me to the nearest sporting goods store. Anyone could see I needed new shoes.

. . .

When I walked into the store in my filthy socks, the two young salesmen met me with worried expressions. It was understandable: in my state, I must have looked like a panhandler come to beg for some shoes. One of them smiled at me anyway. The sight of my Italian leather handbag must have reassured him.

"I want to start jogging."

"Did you lose your shoes, ma'am?"

"No, no. I gave them to someone who needed them."

"Let's see what we can do."

He flashed me the dazzling white smile of a non-coffee-drinker and we proceeded to the back of the store where hundreds of brightly coloured sneakers formed a dizzying mosaic of technical and futuristic brilliance. I sat on a bench to stop my head from spinning.

I took off my socks and put on the ones "Karim, at your service" handed me. Socks all the wannabe joggers slipped on before trying on running shoes – socks theoretically full of fungus, as Jacques, who had an irrational fear of foot diseases, would have said. I pulled them on happily. I liked living on the edge.

"Follow me, let's have you run a bit."

"Run a bit?"

"I need to see how you run to know what kind of shoes you need."

"I just want ordinary running shoes."

"Yes, but I need to analyze your stride in order to give you the right fit, otherwise you might hurt yourself."

"Oh, serious business!"

I went over to the mat and ran back and forth a few times in front of Karim, who, kneeling to examine my stride, had a perfect view of all the flab north of my knees. I'd already self-sabotaged once today, I could handle more. I considered it to be my good deed for the day: tonight he'd find his girl-friend – or boyfriend, for that matter – hotter than ever.

In the end, I learned that I suffered from something called "overpronation." I'd come in to buy running shoes and left with a medical condition. Out of the hundreds of shoes on display, only three would work for me, and all three were hopelessly ugly, awful combinations of neon colours and lines that hinted at aerodynamics. I have nightmares about the revival of eighties fashion, an almost clinical fear. I revelled at the selection.

I was also forced to swallow my usual pride when choosing workout clothes.

"Does the bra fit, ma'am?"

"Uh . . . I think so . . . it's a little tight around my chest . . ."

"That's normal. It's supposed to squeeze your breasts a little. For support."

Squeezed was an understatement; my breasts had been squished into a single shapeless mass. I could have had three or four breasts and no one would have known. My nipples would never again poke through, even when I was cold, unless they tried to go through my back.

"Can you jump a few times, ma'am? That way we'll know if you have enough support."

I'd come this far, so why not? The hinges and lock on the fitting room door shuddered as I jumped – lightly – up and down. The mirror did what it could, but if I kept it up any longer, I'd need a screwdriver. The situation was more ridiculous by the second. I was about to crack up when I realized there might be a camera hidden somewhere. And the sight of me monkeying around on YouTube would finish me off.

Following Karim's advice, I picked out a few articles of high-tech microfibre clothing, including Shock Absorber leggings and a pair of underwear "scientifically proven" for comfort. I'm an easy target for sports marketing: I'll buy anything if science says it works.

"What's great about this pair, ma'am, is that it has strategically placed antibacterial mesh vents."

He was basically telling me with a straight face that I needed to aerate my crotch and butt crack to prevent the proliferation of unwanted germs.

"You can also choose your preferred gluteal support. Over here, we have a range of choices . . ."

"Oh boy!"

"I don't recommend the thong. It's popular with younger women, but more for aesthetics."

"What do women my age usually get?"

"The Firm-Control X-treme."

I wish I'd had the guts to ask him if the underwear he was suggesting compressed backsides as much as the bras compressed boobs, in which case I wouldn't even have a butt crack to have to aerate, but I was scared he would ask me to jump up and down to test the jiggling.

After discussing my most private of parts with a perfect stranger, I walked out of the shop $427 lighter. I needed to run straightaway so I wouldn't regret my purchases. Charlotte was right. Running is free – once you've invested the initial hundreds of dollars.

. . .

Later, once I was in bed – the bed in the guest room – I laughed until I cried as I pictured J.P. trying desperately to hand me back my boots like they were hot potatoes. Then I opened my computer and ordered myself a new pair, also *Made in Italy* if not quite as flashy. I had to give my eyes a chance.

7

In which I ramble on about mundane things

"Do you resent him?"

"Of course I do. A lot."

"Why?"

"*Pfff . . .*"

"Can you try to put it into words?"

The pale pink of her silk button-down had a calming effect. I'd even decided not to time our session. I needed to focus on being efficient and avoid blubbering like a fool.

"The last time we slept together, I didn't know it would be the last time. That's tough to swallow for a woman my age. It might have been my last time ever."

"Would you have wanted to know?"

"I don't see how I could have. 'Hey, Diane, by the way, this is the last time we'll ever have sex . . .'"

"Hmm."

"But he knew, obviously he did. That's what I find so disgusting."

"Why does that disgust you?"

"Because I can picture him saying to himself, 'Come on, Jacques, bang your wife one last time. After that, you're in the clear . . .'"

My voice broke. My chin started to tremble. The pain was never far off, rising in my throat every time I met it head on. My therapist looked deep into my eyes without moving, without speaking. I felt the pain recede, until it was gone. Had it not been for the grace of her non-response, I'd have stopped right there. Big hot tears traced an arc across my cheeks before slipping down my neck.

"I'd like to know what I missed. I want to know how these things happen, how they start, who does what. I know it's silly. This happens to so many people, you hear these stories all the time. But I can't picture how it all started. Everything's so blurry. I just keep playing the same scenes over and over in my head. He gave me a rough idea of when he first started seeing his stupid whore, only because I wouldn't let it go, but I still don't know how it happened. That part is so vague. Why can't he just tell me? If only for the closure. When someone is murdered, their loved ones have the right to know what happened. They're told the weapon that's used, the time of death, whether the person suffered or not. And, if they did, for how long. I'm convinced it's better to know everything, because otherwise you just spend your time speculating. I know, I know, no one died. But picturing that first kiss, the first time their hands touched, it's driving me crazy. Knowing wouldn't change anything, but at least give me somewhere to start hating. I could direct my rage at something specific – the conference, the trip to Boston, the dinner at Buonanotte . . . Because now, it just feels like I've nothing to hold onto, like I'm fumbling around. I picture them at one of those goddamn society parties. Christ, I was so fed up having to fake small talk with people who care only about money. I think of her walking over to him, all glammed up like a starlet, with her big sparkly earrings and kiss-proof lip gloss – so radiant and young, no wrinkles, no bags under her eyes, a goddamn tiny dress over her flat stomach, her tight ass . . . and then I see Jacques looking at her, thinking *oh my God, she's beautiful*, offering to get her a glass of white, chivalrous as a knight in shining armour, how their hands touch, separate, come back together, brush against each other again . . . hands. It's all about the hands. We think it's our eyes that do the talking but I know it's the hands. All it takes is one lingering finger . . . I was never the jealous type, it never really crossed my mind. Well, except for once, a long time ago, but that was all in my head. His colleagues might have noticed, the moment it all started with Charlene, but what do they care? They might have even thought it was funny, everyone does it . . . so many parties and conferences every year, there's always an asshole or two. I could tell you some stories, I swear, but about other people, normally . . . sometimes I picture them in the office together. I imagine Jacques's hand on her shoulder, the beautiful Charlene. 'Come see me in my office, we need to talk about so-and-so's file,' and once the door's closed, someone makes the first move, it doesn't matter who . . . He was supposed to protect us, to push her away, that was *his* job, not hers. She doesn't owe me a thing, he's the one who was supposed to shut it down, and because he didn't, it's like he made the first move . . . Either way, it all boils down to the same thing: I'm the problem. Whether he approached her or just didn't say no when she did, it was because he needed something . . . something that wasn't me. I had no idea he wasn't happy . . ."

The therapist leaned forward a bit and narrowed her eyes, hair cascading over her shoulders.

"Sure, all of a sudden there were lots of meetings that ran late, or he'd go back to the office to pick up a file . . . Once he came home at one in the morning with a coffee from Tim Hortons. He hates their coffee! He got a new credit card for 'client expenses' . . . It could have been just a fling, nothing serious, that I might have understood, to a point . . . but he chose her at the end of the day and that's what kills. He chose her, he chose to give up everything for her, just flushed twenty-eight years of his life down the toilet for a thirty-year-old bimbo, even though he knew it would destroy me. I'm so naïve, *so* naïve, I never thought it could happen to me. I know that's what everyone says, but I really believed it, I'd totally convinced myself . . ."

"Why?"

"Because a part of me always believed those women had it coming to them, at least a little bit. What an idiot I was. In the end, maybe I do deserve it . . . Christ, I thought it was all so beneath me."

She wasn't writing anything down. I was blubbering on, no doubt recounting the same inanities as every woman who'd ever ended up in a puddle on her couch, holding their guts in their hands. I wasn't reinventing the pain, I was living it. I was working through it like everyone else, had the same thoughts and fears – no need to waste any ink, I agreed with her. It was the same thing, *the same fucking thing.*

"I thought everything we'd been through made us stronger, made us steadfast, brought us closer, but now I think it just wore us out. Maybe it isn't good to know your partner too well, maybe it adds to the distance rather than shrinking it . . . Over the years you keep hearing the same stories, you keep having to deal with the same habits, and the flaws just seem to get bigger . . . I know I got on his nerves sometimes . . . I don't know what comes first, you fall in love with someone else because you're sick of your wife, or you fall in love and *then* get sick of her? Like the chicken and the egg. I'm ashamed, which is weird . . . he's the one who dumped me and I'm the one who's ashamed. I feel like everyone's looking at me like I have the plague. I tell myself they must think Jacques had his reasons for leaving me, that I must be boring or unbearable to live with. Maybe he just stayed for the kids – lots of people do. Charlotte did just move out, it's probably not a coincidence . . . I'm ashamed and I feel dirty. I take scalding hot baths every night and scrub so hard it's like I'm trying to take off a layer of my skin, but it doesn't help . . ."

I scratched my arm and glanced at my watch: we were thirteen minutes over time.

"I feel bad for you, you must hear the same stories over and over . . ."

"Your wounds are fresh. If you broke your arm, it wouldn't hurt any less to know millions of other people have broken their arms, too."

"If you look at it like that . . ."

8

In which I recall the joys of adolescence

THE NOTION THAT I was somehow responsible for my situation came to me partly because of what I'd observed of Claudine's family: her daughters gave her such a hard time you'd think they wanted her to pay for the plight of humanity. And as with so many stories of this kind, she refused to vilify or accuse Philippe of anything while he had a field day justifying his decision to leave, with all the badmouthing you'd expect. He all but blamed her for global warming.

In her infinite wisdom, Claudine clung to the belief that sooner or later her kids would figure out the real story and eventually make amends for their cruel and unwarranted behaviour. But as she waited for the blessed day to come, her two daughters made her life hell. They were perfectly comfortable acting obnoxiously when I was around, treating me like a piece of furniture. At thirteen and sixteen, they reminded me of Nelly, the little brat from *Little House on the Prairie*.

"Where are my leggings?"

"Everything's hanging in the laundry room."

"Are my leggings there?"

"Go check."

"I bet they're not even there."

"If you did your own laundry, you'd know where your stuff is."

"Screw you!"

Laurie walked away in grumbling. Another missed opportunity for a good kick in the ass.

"Laurie, get back here this instant!"

"I don't have time, I need to find my clothes."

"Get back here now!"

"No! I'm sick of your stupid lectures!"

"Oh yeah? Well, you're grounded! You hear me? No going out tonight!"

"Like I care! I'm going out tonight anyway!"

"If you put one foot outside, I'm cancelling your cell phone plan!"

"You do that and I'll call Dad. He'll stop paying alimony! And he's the one who pays for my cell anyway."

"That little shit! I'm going to skin her alive."

Claudine's younger daughter, Adèle, had just walked into the kitchen looking her usual exhausted, jaded self. She dragged herself over to the nearest chair and let her world-weary body plop down in an almost liquid *sploosh*. If it hadn't been for her awful paper-thin crop top and blue highlights, she could have passed for someone who'd spent weeks fleeing a war-torn country on foot. She rested her head on her arms.

"There's nothing to do."

"What do you mean, nothing to do? Call Léa!"

"She's at her dad's. It's like, on the other side of the world."

"What about Noémie?"

"Ugh, I don't feel like it."

"Why not?"

"Her little sister never leaves us alone."

"Then tell her to come over here."

"No, it's too lame here."

Their father's house had a finished basement, a swimming pool, a hot tub, an impossible array of electronic devices, and walls of screens for projecting movies, like in *Fahrenheit 451*. Claudine downed her half-glass of white in a single gulp. She could have used something stronger.

"What about everything we bought the other week so you could learn to draw manga?"

"Don't feel like it."

"Then go take a bike ride, it's beautiful out."

"*Yuck!*"

"You could make me another friendship bracelet. I lost mine."

"Lost" was one way to put it. The last one Adèle made had shades of orange and brown with a small lime green thread running through it, an eyesore that "accidentally" came apart.

"You could make me a nice one with a black and red design."

"Making bracelets is for babies."

"Oh, so that's how it is, we're babies now? Then go to the park."

"You just want me to leave you guys alone."

"I just want you to find something to do. To live a little instead of being a vegetable."

"But there's nothing to do . . ."

"Then go take a nap, that'll pass the time. You look like you're starting to rot, anyway."

"I don't feel like it."

I knocked back my drink and handed the glass to Claudine in solidarity. When the enemy is in your kitchen, you've got to use the means at hand to defend yourself.

"You know, it's funny. I don't remember ever being bored when I was her age," Claudine said to me, dramatically.

Adèle rolled her eyes. "You're lucky."

"Oh! I know what you could do with Noémie," continued Claudine. "Did you ever make prank calls, Diane?"

"Did I ever!"

"It's easy – you go through the phone book and pick random people to call, then say stupid things."

"The *phone book*?" said Adèle, appalled.

"Look online, then. Call people you know, or ones you don't. Like guys from school. Pretend you're another girl from school and try to play a practical joke."

"We used to get pizzas delivered to our teachers' houses," I added.

"Oh my God, that's right! Pizza!"

"That's so dumb!"

We started tapping into the folklore of our good ideas, ruses that were popular back in the day – before the whole me-myself-and-I attitude completely revolutionized the art of teen entertainment. Kids today want to be as visible as possible; back then, we did everything we could to slip away unnoticed.

"You could throw eggs onto people's sheds. They cook in a second on a black roof."

"It's funnier on cars."

"Or throw water balloons off the overpass!"

"Yes!"

"It's hilarious! When the police show up, you just play dumb. Say that you saw it on *Funniest Home Videos*."

"Or if you want something tamer, you could do the run-away five-dollar bill. You hook a five-dollar bill to some fishing line and put it in the middle of the sidewalk, then tug on the line when someone tries to pick it up. I'll give you a fiver. It'll crack you up, you'll see."

"That reminds me of the butt prints."

"I don't know that one."

"No? It's so funny. You pee in your pants, then sit on the sidewalk to make prints of your butt cheeks. You make a trail for as long as you're able to pee."

"Not bad! And there's always the classic brown bag on the porch."

"The brown bag . . ."

"You poop in a paper bag, then put it on the front steps of someone you don't like, someone who really pisses you off – except for us, we don't count – then you light the bag on fire and ring the doorbell so that the person who answers jumps on it to put out the fire. There'll be poop everywhere!"

"The problem is that you have to need to poop."

"True. That's the catch."

"We used to change road signs around with black and white tape. We'd change street names – 'Hartland' to 'Fartland' – or we'd change one-way arrows into big penises. You just have to round off the points to make the head."

"Okay, you guys are totally nuts," said Adèle in disgust.

"Wait, we've got loads of other ideas! What about frogs? If you put a cigarette in their mouths, they'll explode!"

"I'm going to Noémie's."

"Aw, too bad! We could've gone with you to egg some cars . . ."

Just then Laurie breezed by, her damp leggings clinging to her legs.

"Where do you think you're going?"

"Somewhere."

"I told you, you're grounded!"

"Whatever!"

The glass in the china cabinet rattled and clinked as the door slammed. Claudine calmly got out of her seat, picked up her phone, and searched for a number in her contacts.

"Yes, hello. I'd like to suspend service for one of the numbers on my account . . . yes . . . uh-huh . . . I have a family plan, and I want to block my daughter's number as soon as possible . . . yes, I'm Claudine Poulin. Can you block it remotely? Yes, until further notice . . . yes . . . the reason? Well, do you have options? For being impolite, rude . . . conflict? Sure, that works . . ."

She hung up just as Adèle slipped back into the kitchen, a little bag over her shoulder.

"Let us know if you need some ideas, honey."

And the door slammed a second time. Claudine rubbed her hands together.

"Right, let's get out of here."

"Where to?"

"Anywhere, as long as it's not here."

"We can't drive. We've had too much to drink . . ."

"There's a little pub a few streets over."

"Aren't we too old for places like that?"

"Of course not, it's full of people our age!"

"Okay. Don't forget your phone."

"I'm not taking it. Pain in the ass!"

As we walked out the door, the next-door neighbour was calling her cat. "Here, kitty, kitty! Come here, baby, come on! Here, little kitty! Come to Mummy!"

Solitude can do that to you. Physically, she looked just like us.

"I know what you're thinking."

"What?"

"About the girls."

"I'm not! I know what teenagers are like. I've had a few."

Nevertheless, the scenes I had just witnessed made me want to call Jacques and thank him for waiting until the kids left home to throw me out like an old sock.

"The girls are furious. Having two homes in two different cities really pisses them off."

"Are they like that with Philippe, too?"

"I'd say so. Last week, he told Laurie she'd better start acting nicer to his girlfriend because if he had to choose between the two of them, Laurie was not at the top of his list."

"Are you serious?"

"Ms. Uncooperative must have really laid it on thick. Philippe even warned me he was 'taking steps' to kick her out until she 'shaped up.' You think the prick would realize it's his job to shape her up, but no! He just wants her out."

"He can't do that!"

"Oh, whatever Philippe wants, Philippe gets."

"What about you?"

"What can I do? Tell him I don't want her, either? Give him yet another reason to hate me? No, I take the fall for both of us. Laurie has to be in a good mood at her dad's, has to play the happy kid in a new home. It never crossed his mind the girls might get bent out of shape, that wasn't part of the plan. But of course that's not his fault, oh no!"

"Would Adèle stay at his place alone?"

"I doubt it. Besides, when Philippe learns she's this close to being expelled from school, I bet he'll find an appropriate punishment. Something like 'I'm throwing you out too, but it's for your own good. Come back when you've smartened up.'"

"What's going on at school?"

"She doesn't give a shit. Laurie's on the warpath, and Adèle's a blob of Jell-O. They kick you out once you fail three classes – unless you make a generous donation to the football team."

"That makes me sick."

The bar was bursting with people gathered together over drinks. The air felt thick and heavy as molasses. Body odour fused with the smell of fermenting liquid being consumed in small sips to dilute the week's miseries.

We settled in at the bar and watched a tall leggy girl with thick bangs pace back and forth behind it. She had a selfie pout and a tattoo of a woodcutter on her arm. You'd have to travel back to the eighties to see fashion impose itself so relentlessly. And no, don't try it: nothing looks more average nowadays than a sleeve of tattoos.

A large mirror above the bar reflected the crowd getting drunk behind us. They were younger – a lot younger – no offence to Claudine, who'd included anyone legally able to drink in her "people our age" just so that I'd come.

When the bartender finally came over to serve us, he pointed his beard at us in a quick nod that I took to be an abridged form of "Good evening, ladies. What can I get for you?" Nobody bothers with pleasantries anymore, time is too precious. Claudine raised two fingers and said "White" without smiling. Efficient.

We solved a few of the world's problems and asked for as many rounds, twirling our fingers in the air with a "One more time!" We drafted a few not-so-radical public policies, spewed vomit on our exes with abandon, settled accounts with two or three hopelessly incompetent colleagues, laid the foundation for a new – anti-Heideggerian – direction in philosophy, the details still to be ironed out, and quietly lamented our lives and all their terrifically disappointing moments.

Just like he'd done every night since Jacques had left, Antoine texted me to make sure I was okay. And for once, I didn't lie: "I'm great, sweetie. I'm with Claudine. Mum xxx." I know you don't have to sign a text, but I love writing the word "Mum."

I waited a bit too long to go to the bathroom – so long that, once I was on my feet, I wasn't sure I'd be able to hold it all in. I called on the few neurons that weren't completely sloshed in alcohol and mustered up the nerve to get in line for the bathroom. I waited, contracting all my sphincters as hard as I was able to avoid the humiliation of wetting my pants in the ultra-trendy bar.

When it was my turn, I scurried into the stall doing my best to pretend that there was no hurry. It only took another second and a half to show the girls in line that women my age have everything under control. I didn't notice the big wad of shit and toilet paper clogging the bowl until I'd already lowered my cheeks onto the seat. I had no choice but to leave my own addition, since I was unable to contain my bladder any longer. I lifted my bottom a few inches to avoid being splashed as the drops bounced up from the pile of excrement. I'd have preferred a porta potty in some faraway field.

Like everyone before me, I left casually and hid my crime by avoiding eye contact. Given the amount of paper, it was clear I wasn't the cause of the problem. I'd only augmented it – which, all things considered, isn't really a crime. Or an excuse.

Once I'd sat back down, I couldn't contain my laughter as I told Claudine what had happened.

"Shit! Who's going to unclog it?"

"By the look of it, they'll need an axe!"

My cell phone rang. I didn't recognize the number. "I don't answer if I don't know who it is."

"Same here."

"That's why prank calls don't work anymore."

The fifth time it rang, I took the call, ready to give whoever it was a piece of my mind.

"Hello?"

"Where are you guys?"

"Who's this?"

"Laurie."

"Laurie?"

Claudine slapped her forehead.

"Here we go. The little princess must be royally pissed off."

"Where are you?"

"We went out for a drink."

"Where?"

"At Chez Louis."

"No! Don't tell her!" But she'd already hung up.

"Sorry about that."

"She'll come waltzing in here, just you wait! With no phone on a Friday night . . ."

"You think she'll show up here?"

"How much do you want to bet?"

"Maybe she was worried. We didn't say where we were going."

"Hah! That's a good one. Worried!"

Claudine was still laughing when I saw Laurie's reflection in the bar mirror.

"Uh-oh! We've got company."

Laurie hustled our way, parting the crowd like a bionic swimmer. She stopped just short of her mother. I glanced at her hands to make sure she wasn't concealing a blunt object, maybe a brick or a flashlight.

"Why didn't you take your phone with you?"

"I didn't feel like lishening to you whine. You're grounded, you know that."

Claudine's lips, numbed by alcohol, stumbled over the words. I flashed an idiotic, happy smile to show Laurie I had her mother's back – that we were in the same boat, guilty of the same crime.

"You need to come home, Mum."

"Nooo! I'm shtaying here. No one's bothering me, I'm good."

"Mum, please come."

I could sense the storm approaching. Claudine was clutching her glass, the golden liquid sloshing against the sides as it swirled.

"Mad about your phone, baby girl?"

"Your brother wants to talk to you."

"Hah! My brother? Mr. Me-Me-Me? Must be in deep shit."

"Come on."

"What did he say?"

"Come."

"First, temme what's going on."

"Not here."

"Then I'm not leaving."

"Your dad died."

Claudine hadn't spoken to her father since her divorce. He'd blamed her for everything, claiming she'd been too "emasculating." By his logic, which reeked of machismo, the woman is always the one responsible for breaking up a family. A product of another generation touting ideas of the Almighty Man, he couldn't see the clearly medieval attitude in his point of view. In fact, he never missed the opportunity to lay it on thick, declaring that men strayed because

Mother Nature commanded them to reproduce until the very end – unlike women, who dry up long before kicking the bucket and are thus saved from the torment of desire. Clearly an agreeable fellow with a penchant for biology.

Love and hate didn't mix well with alcohol.

"He pissed me off right to the very end, the old bastard," slurred Claudine.

Claudine's brother André was just as unpleasant, though of an entirely different breed. He was a master manipulator who suffered from innumerable undiagnosed conditions: navel-gazing, narcissism, a god complex, mythomania, acute actor-itis, cash drain, compulsive lying, etc. Claudine had saved his ass more than once, clearing up his nebulous debts. She'd eventually had to leave him to his fate, to avoid being pulled down with him. But death attracts scavengers, and he was back.

We walked slowly back to Claudine's house in the pouring rain, letting the water wash over us. She restrained everything she could: her mood, her hair, her clothes. Laurie didn't say a word about her phone. She even hooked her mother's arm with her own so they could walk together. Adolescence might end one day, after all. We could only hope.

9

In which, like Rocky,
I scream "Charleeeeene!"

Darling Jacques's darling Charlene wanted to meet me and talk, woman to woman. *Blah, blah, blah.* She wanted to give me the "I'm *so* sorry" song and dance. Movies, books, and "chicklit" are rife with pity-party scenes like these, in which the evil mistress – too pretty, too young, and always a little stupid – begs forgiveness from the woman who's been discarded, with a sincerity as authentic as her fake tits, in order to clear her own conscience. They want to have their cake and eat it – along with the guy who makes it, too. No doubt she wanted me to realize, listening to her story, that it wasn't her fault, they'd only succumbed to some greater force of symbiotic alchemy that united them and transcended – or rather, annulled – all past promises. But there was no chance of this happening; she didn't have the vocabulary to express complex ideas and there was no way I was about to forgive her. Even if I wasn't actually interested in revenge, it would feel good to stuff a little of my hate and pain into the back corner of their minds.

I agreed to meet Charlene only because she'd artfully assured me over the phone that she hadn't run the idea past Jacques, who wouldn't have approved. *Top secret*, she'd purred, and so I'd been offered a chance to cheat on Jacques with his very own mistress – if without (much) physical contact. I hoped to find out things only she could tell me: here was an opportunity to study the cyclone from the inside.

Charlene's Secrets

She showed up wearing neither high heels nor a Bardot-inspired scarf. No, she'd come in loungewear for me to know right off the bat that this was a gesture of friendship and that I could laugh at her a bit if I wanted. It was generous of her, I'll admit. I'd expected her to waltz in decked out in business attire – an intimidating pantsuit, matching stilettos, tasteful jewellery – but she'd opted for a natural look: grey cotton, run-of-the-mill sandals, and a pallid complexion without a trace of make-up. It's really tough to go after someone in loungewear, they already seem so down on their luck. Bailiffs and meter maids should seriously consider the look.

I'd invited her over for drinks in the yard so she'd be able to cry unabashedly (not appropriate in a restaurant) and tell me whatever nonsense she wanted. It had rained overnight, so I'd towelled off two chairs. When she arrived, obviously I made the mistake of offering her a third chair that was soaked. She wasn't wearing the beige linen pants I'd hoped for, but it still made a nice dark stain and the fabric stuck to buttocks you could tell – even in loungewear – were very toned. I mumbled an apology and held out the right chair. She played the game and sat down, offering heartfelt compliments.

"Your house is so beautiful!"

"Thank you."

"I love what you've done with the backyard."

"Oh, that was all Jacques. He should be able to do something nice with your place."

"And the great deck you guys have!"

"The deck *I* have."

"Oh, right. Sorry."

"Mr. Nelligan did it. He's a friend of Jacques's."

"Oh? I'll have to remember that."

What a bitch. I wanted to empty the contents of the water pitcher over her head then and there. I'd set it on the table as a precaution and purposely forgot the glasses, of course, fully intending to throw it at her. But all my excitement had waned when she showed up looking so unkempt. Suddenly it seemed unreasonable to waste a couple of litres of water when there was no possibility of ruining a hairdo, a leather jacket, or skilfully applied make-up.

"If you only knew what it took for me to come here today . . ."

Cue the tears. She opened her eyes wide, fanning them with her hand as if to dry them. Fascinating. Here was Charlene Dugal sobbing like a cow in my beautifully landscaped backyard, a situation I craved about as much as I did a slice of ham and pineapple pizza. I was careful not to put a friendly hand on her shoulder, I'd have been tempted to strangle her.

"This was supposed to be a quick chat, Charlene. What did you want to talk about?"

"Sorry, I'm sorry . . . I . . . I wanted to tell you I under-stand what you're going through. I didn't mean for this to happen. It happened to me once, too . . ."

What *she* had been through didn't interest me one bit. Let Francis Cabrel write a song about it. I wanted to know where things stood between them, what their plans were. Jacques turned into a limp fish whenever I asked about his plans. He was evasive about everything, keeping everything annoyingly veiled in mystery. I figured it was his way of buying time but also of sparing me. And I had to be honest; beneath the lay-ers of bitterness I'd built up, a measure of hope lay dormant, enough to pull me back from the edge and condemn me to believing that eventually Jacques just might come back. It was obviously a survival mechanism, and I knew it was ridiculous no matter how comforting it felt. "I wanted you to know that . . . I . . . *sniff* . . . *sniff, sniff* . . . that I didn't mean for this to happen . . ." *Blah, blah, blah.*

And then, I heard a bit more of their story through a series of tear-soaked sentences chopped into barely intelligible words that nonetheless helped reconstruct the all-too-inevitable facts – a chance meeting . . . a vulnerable moment . . . cocktails . . . the conference . . . hands . . . confusion . . . surprise . . . guilt . . . no, yes, maybe . . . heart . . . marriage . . . love . . . fallacious (or fellatio, I didn't quite catch that one) . . . respect . . . life . . . love at first sight . . . chemistry (fucking chemistry!) . . . the lot punctuated with "you knows" probably intended to give a touch of humanity to her pathetic account. Obviously, and in summary, she had been Jacques's mistress for some time before our separation. Just as I suspected, thank you very much.

She'd not stopped producing a steady stream of mucus that was blocking her nose and constricting her throat as she gasped for air, and since I was making no effort to help, she ended by asking to use the bathroom. Her face covered by one hand, she indicated with the other that I should remain seated, which suited me just fine. She walked into the house and turned left, not hesitating for a moment, as if she lived there. I tried to repel the scenarios running through my head – she'd been in my house before, the tramp! – and focus gleefully on imagining her in my paper-free bathroom. (I had gone into both bathrooms and purposely removed all the toilet paper, tissues, towels, tampons, washcloths, and any other accessory that might help mop up tears, snot, pee – or, even better, poop.) She was not about to wipe her little ass on the glass shower door. Those last few drops of moisture – or whatever else might exit her body – would end up in her underwear.

As luck would have it, in her distress she'd left her purse on the ground next to her chair. No backup tissues to the rescue.

She seemed to have pulled herself together by the time she came back. She'd suddenly run out of time and needed to cut short our long-awaited conversation.

"I think I'd better get going."

"Already? We barely had time to chat."

"Really, I have to go."

Everything about her eagerness to leave annoyed me. Her shifty eyes, her halting tone; the violence with which her hands tried to force an elegant pleat in her clothing. She clearly wasn't used to such casual clothes. I couldn't figure out which part of her outfit she'd used to blow her nose; she must have shot her snot into the sink like a lumberjack, then flushed it away with a great rush of water. It was a good thing she wanted to leave; a few minutes more and I'd have been at her throat. I hated her, passionately, not as much for stealing my husband as for this meeting designed to absolve her of the guilt casting a shadow over her new happiness. As if she'd forgotten it was directly related to my *unhappiness*. She'd taken everything from me and yet, feigning a few tears and sincerity, she wanted me to grant her inner peace. She could take her sincerity and shove it up her ass.

"So you've been here a few times?"

"Here? What do you mean, 'here'?"

"Here, in my house – what used to be our house."

"Of course not! What are you talking about?"

"You knew where the bathroom was."

"It's not rocket science . . . houses all resemble each other."

"No, no, they don't."

"Well, pretty much."

"You didn't hesitate for a second."

"I think I'd better leave. I don't like the way things are going."

"I'll walk you out."

Once I was up, I could feel it was the right moment – the beige leather seats of her Mini Cooper could use a little shower. So, in one deft motion, I emptied the pitcher of cold water down her back without even pretending it was an accident. She screamed and ran away. I bet she was worried I had a dozen eggs under the table. I kicked myself for not having thought of it earlier.

The car sped away, burning rubber and sending dust flying. I shouted something approaching a compliment to officially mark the end of our friendly conversation. "You look great in sweats!"

Then I closed my eyes and tried to picture her wriggling in discomfort, her clothes soggy with water and pee sticking to the car's expensive leather interior. I congratulated myself on the extent of the damage I'd managed with, all things considered, so little water.

I stood there for a moment in front of the house, empty pitcher in hand, and heart racing with adrenaline, ready to explode. Mrs. Nadaud, poorly hidden behind her living room curtain, was enjoying the impromptu show that, while not spectacular, at least offered the magic of live action. She didn't return the greeting I called out, to avoid giving herself away. So, for her and all my other secret admirers hidden behind a window or door of their tidy little house, I shouted as loudly as I could, "That's Charlene, my husband's mistress! She's the one Jacques left me for! She's got one hell of an ass, eh?"

I waited for a reaction that never came. It occurred to me it was a good day to try out my overpriced running gear. I had a pair of sneakers and a heart full of rage. The rest would come naturally.

10

In which I try to run

AFTER CHARLENE LEFT, INVIGORATED by my minor freak-out and kitted out as a professional runner – minus the GPS watch ("Let me think about it," I'd told Karim) – I headed to the park for my very first run since grade ten. During the week I'd taken care to read up on the basics online. Everything would be fine; I just needed to start out slow, not push the pace, and drink lots of water. I'd get in shape *and* clear my head.

After two or three hundred metres, it's hard to say (I was already regretting not buying the GPS watch), a sharp stitch pierced my left side. Just like every time I'd gone running in high school. (In college, I'd taken meditation classes and fencing.) I kept going, taking deep breaths in and out: I'd read that it would eventually pass. Just before reaching the playground, I felt a second stitch, this one stronger and more painful, beneath my right breast. I slowed down but did not stop, holding myself with both hands and massaging the knots as hard as I could to try and break them up. It would pass if I just kept taking deep breaths. It said so online.

By the time the water fountain came into view, it felt like my ribcage was about to explode and spew guts everywhere.

My temples were throbbing unusually fast, I was whistling through my nose, I was sweating out of every orifice, and my hands and feet were swollen – all sure signs of imminent death. When I remembered that I hadn't updated my will since Jacques left, I stopped short.

"Shit! No *way* he's getting his hands on my money that easily! *No way!* Bring on the flab and fuck the four hundred bucks of running gear."

A group of girls cut across the grass to avoid me. I'd have done the same thing: a madwoman with bloodshot eyes talking to herself is a scary thing. It doesn't matter when or where.

I should have been sweating, but mostly I was furious. My body was turning against me when all I wanted was to take care of it, make up for lost time, and give it a chance to be desirable once again. Such ingratitude.

I flipped the finger at every curtain that swayed as I walked home and set to work as soon as I was through my front door. I moved some furniture – mostly things Jacques had left behind – out of the second-floor window. In pieces. I figured it would help the house breathe a bit. Rooms, like bodies, need oxygen. I was already on a roll, so I called the detective Claudine had recommended.

A little later, Charlotte arrived in a bit of a panic.

"Mum? There you are! What the heck are you doing?"

"Oh, hi! What a nice surprise! I'm just doing a little cleaning."

97

"Mum, you've got to stop destroying the house!"

"I have too much stuff."

"We can give the furniture away. Post online and it'll be gone in a second."

"Okay, I'll stop. I just needed to get the blood flowing."

"You went running?"

"Eh, not really. It didn't work."

"You've got to alternate between running and walking when you start."

"Ah."

"You tried to run, just like that?"

"Kind of."

"Let's make a date for this week. We'll go running together."

"I think I'm a lost cause, sweetie."

"Anyone can run, Mum. I'll make you a little workout schedule."

"So, what, you were in the area?"

"No, Dad called."

"Your *father* called you?"

"Charlene came home totally freaking out."

"Oh, it was just a little water."

"Mum . . ."

"I dropped the pitcher."

"Everyone's been trying to reach you."

"Why?"

"We were worried."

"Oh, come on . . ."

"Even Dad."

"Oh really! Him?"

"He wasn't too happy when he found out Charlene had gone to see you."

"I invited her over, the idiot."

"She's not an idiot, she's curious. It's normal."

"She came in sweats so I'd feel sorry for her."

When Charlotte put her hand on my arm, my eyes filled with tears. They slid down the runway of my cheekbones before taking the plunge and dropping to the floor. My head was spinning from the strain of everything I could no longer manage.

"But what about you, how are you doing, sweetheart? We're always talking about me."

"I'm pretty good."

"Oh yeah? Is something up?"

"Dom's back."

"He is? No way! I knew it! I told you, didn't I?"

"Yeah, you were right."

"What are you going to do?"

"I don't know. I think I might keep him guessing a little."

"Just a little."

"Just because."

"You still love him. Don't lose him."

"Dad says that getting back with an ex is like putting on dirty socks."

I tried not to focus on the fact that I was the dirty sock in this analogy. But still, as a precaution, I put down the sledgehammer I was holding.

"Tell him dirty socks can be washed."

Jacques would never warm up to Dominic, an artist with a bohemian streak and none of the same values as him. Dominic lived by an upside-down version of Maslow's hierarchy of needs, which was unsettling for an engineer like Jacques, who had both feet on the ground. Without a "noble" profession and money of his own, there could be no salvation of Dominic in the eyes of my ex-husband, my pair of dirty socks.

"Don't tell your grandmother. She'll give you a long lecture about the ideal man."

"Want to hear something that'll cheer you up?"

"Sure."

"Grandma hates Charlene."

"Well, what do you know, maybe she's improving with age."

11

In which I try to find the pet store

"VULNERABLE?"

"Yes, but it's hard to describe. It's like I've forgotten how things work."

"What do you mean?"

"I feel like I've gotten worse as a mother."

"Why is that?"

"I don't feel as grounded or as sure of myself. Like a chair with only three legs."

Her eyebrows shot up, just as they did each time she wanted me to continue.

"When Charlotte was little, maybe three or four, she used to have terrible anxiety for a kid her age. It started with the pet store. We were driving home one night when suddenly she started crying for no reason. I looked at her through the rear-view mirror, my baby girl in her car seat, her little fists rubbing her eyes. I asked why she was crying, and she told me she didn't know where the pet store was. 'But why do you need to know that, sweetie?' 'Because I want a cat when I grow up,' she said. 'Well, I know where the pet store is, and I'll tell you.' Charlotte was crazy about cats – she'd wanted one so badly, poor thing, but Jacques wouldn't hear of it. He even told her she was allergic so he didn't have to be the bad guy. She calmed down a bit, I thought we were done with it, but a few minutes later she started to cry again. 'What's going on, pumpkin?' 'I can't get to the pet store if I don't have a car.' 'I'll bring you in mine. We'll go together, honey. I'll go with you, don't worry. I'll be there, I've got a car, I know where the store is, everything's fine, you don't have to cry . . .' She started sobbing again. 'But Mum, we only have one car seat and I'm going to have two kids.'"

"Wow!"

"At the time, it was hard not to laugh – she'd clearly thought her plan through. I told her we'd buy another car seat, that I knew where to get one, and that I had enough money for the cat, the car seat, and anything else we needed, that I knew how to take care of cats, and babies, and lots of other things. I could tell it wasn't so much what I said, but how I said it that was calming her down. 'Don't worry, Charlotte. I'm here, I'll always be here. And I know everything you need to know.'"

"Hmm."

"I didn't doubt myself for a second. I knew where I was going, why I did the things I did, it was all clear to me. I had a retirement plan and trips in mind, I knew exactly what we'd be eating on any given day, what I'd plant in the garden come summer . . . Now all my plans are in tatters, I can't think beyond the night ahead, and nothing ever works out. I've got to make new plans, but I just can't, I don't feel like it. I could go to bed and sleep for ten years."

"These things take time, it's normal."

"I wanted to be strong for the kids. I wanted them to come home if they needed advice or comfort, if they needed a break from life's problems or just some spaghetti sauce."

"And they can't do that anymore?"

"It's like the roles are reversed. I'm the one who's fragile, who's hurting, the one having a hard time. I'm not certain of anything anymore. It feels like I have to start all over again and I just don't know where to begin. I don't even know where the pet store is anymore."

12

In which I witness a scene
worthy of *The Twilight Zone*

O F MY TOP TEN list of least favourite events to attend, baby showers are first, followed by weddings and baptisms (a tie), and funerals.

The funeral of Mr. Poulin, Claudine's father, was held just off the highway in an imitation stone castle – a façade of fake stone concealing walls that were really made of wood. In keeping with the building's artificial nature, the plants lining the lobby were bathed in natural light but just as fake.

In Room B, which was reserved for the Poulin funeral – "*to your right, all the way down, by the bathrooms, ma'am*" – family, friends, and strangers formed little circles of discussion on a carpet with spiral motifs in shades of dizzying purple. I tried to maintain my gaze at shoulder-level.

Most guests were older and wore appropriately funereal attire, save one woman mysteriously outfitted head to toe in an absolutely fascinating sparkly emerald-green ensemble. She even had matching eye shadow. She was laughing and chatting animatedly, waving her arms about while the others clutched their water glasses solemnly. A spot of cheer in a sea of grey. I made some mental notes for my own funeral arrangements: invite people to dress colourfully, and have it be a mini-ceremony in some dimly lit bar with no speeches, and make sure the wine flows freely.

I made the rounds, going up to all official mourners. "Hi, I'm Diane. I'm a friend of Claudine's. I'm sorry for your loss." I must have said this a good twenty times, adjusting the degree of my earnestness and body language to each mourner's apparent grief. With André the Hypocrite Brother, I forced a fake smile and was sure to remove "I'm sorry for your loss" from the equation. I saw no reason to make even the slightest apology and, instead, swallowed all the insults I wanted to hurl his way. That was already generous enough.

I turned to Claudine, her face swollen with sadness, and gathered her up in my arms like a flesh-eating plant. The eternal falling-out to which her father's death condemned her only added to the bitterness of her cocktail of daily struggles. Laurie thanked me for coming with a firm handshake. She'd grown up fast. Clearly, Adèle had not: she was sitting at a distance, exhausted from standing up for all of thirty minutes. No Royal Canadian Mounted Police for her. Claudine's mother, at eighty-three, looked a hell of a lot better. Philippe, in his capacity as ex-son-in-law, stood at the very back of the receiving line. I managed to avoid him without making a show of it. I bet he was thanking me on the inside.

The ceremony, once underway, alternated between songs, family speeches, and words from the officiant, who delivered a hollow sermon around the metaphor of the four seasons. It was all going smoothly up to that point, a total snooze-fest as is the custom. The fun started when Claudine's sister Claire, ten years her junior, started to speak. She was in the process of listing off all the extraordinary things her dad had taught her (how to skate, use a baseball glove, wash the car, wax the car, etc.) when a raspy voice sounded loudly from the middle of the room.

"I wouldn't thank him too much, if I were you . . ."

Claire paused, then continued. Guests started to murmur into the ears of their neighbours.

". . . every Saturday morning, Dad, you would show me your tools in the garage . . ."

"If it'd been up to him, you wouldn't be here!"

A miniscule old woman was standing up, pointing a finger toward the ceiling as if she were calling a witness.

"He didn't want you!"

The people around her tried to calm her down. Another old woman – even tinier, if possible – was pulling on her sleeve to try to make her sit down. A young woman held her firmly by the shoulders.

"Auntie, stop that, now's not the time."

"It sure as hell is! He's *dead*!"

"Exactly. What good can it do?"

"The man had no heart! If we don't say so now, it'll never be said!"

Several people tried, gently, to usher her to the door, nudging her to take tiny steps in the right direction. But the mini-woman was like a geyser. With twisted, feeble hands, she pushed back at those trying to lead her away. She'd been sitting on her story for forty years and the stopper had finally come loose.

"He wanted an abortion!"

I grabbed one of the glasses on the table next to me to sniff its contents: water. Every person in the room was thinking, "She must have forgotten to take her meds," "Maybe it's a blood clot," "She's half senile," and the like. But it hardly mattered; her cry rang true in a room knit by hypocrisy.

Claire sought refuge in her husband's arms. All of a sudden, she was no longer inspired to sing the praises of a dead man who – in a manner no one could have anticipated – had just been raked across the coals. The little scandal flitted across everyone's lips in a hubbub that started to conflate uncontrollably. The officiant scrambled to the microphone and hushed the crowd with an indifferent, "pay no heed" expression, so that the ceremony could continue. Likely this was not the first such incident she'd witnessed – death is fertile ground for settling scores. Behind her, the scene altogether surreal, Claudine's mother was laughing – or rather, trying not to laugh. She was managing very badly, her shoulders were shaking and her face, twisted into a wrinkled little raisin, seemed about to burst.

Next to her, a gentleman who looked to be around a hundred handed her a handkerchief so she could hide her face. It was confusing; it was easy to believe she was crying but the damage was done. The atmosphere in the room swung between discomfort and nervous laughter. Those who knew the truth stared at the floor, and others who, like me, had heard whisperings of her father's infidelities – Claudine even had a half-brother somewhere out West – found it amusing that a woman who'd suffered so much could exact her revenge with a few good laughs over her husband's coffin.

Claudine's brother had reserved himself the pleasure of delivering his eulogy at the very end of the ceremony, like a keynote speaker with top billing. He lived up to the image Claudine had painted of him.

He began his homage by recounting *his* birth, followed by his first steps, *his* first time skating, his first time on a bike, *his* first injuries, etc., effortlessly delivered, like a seasoned politician tasked with putting a crowd to sleep. Some of the uncles laughed, their Adam's apples bouncing, convinced of their truth despite having no recollection of these episodes. André had been careful to skim off the cream of his life, leaving the chunks of his disgracefully misguided youth in the sieve – a dishonest biographer could not have done better – as he casually intertwined anecdotes of his own life with those of his father's.

"When I looked up at my dad watching me play ball from the stands of Parc Saint-Roch, I knew he was happy." After twenty minutes of such an inspirational account, the lady in sequins loudly articulated the malaise most of us were feeling.

"My God, he's getting one hell of a roast, isn't he?"

Guests within a radius several feet around her allowed themselves a good laugh. One of the old uncles took advantage of the fissure that had just opened up. "Ah come on, he'll be at it for a while yet! It's his father, for chrissake!" Not about to back down, André was winding up to deliver another platitude when Laurie crept up behind him, grabbed the cord of the microphone, and pulled with all her might. The plug came out of the socket in a flurry of sparks. A cold shower of silence fell over the crowd.

Claudine's mother burst out laughing again, this time without restraint. I'd be willing to bet the woman hadn't been so entertained in ages.

One of the funeral directors found the perfect words to restore the peace: "Ladies and gentlemen, sandwiches are being served in the back room." In an instant the crowd was congregating at the far door, moving together like a school of fish. Speeches, fireworks, and a buffet: the funeral was a success.

I was making my way over to congratulate Laurie and hug Claudine before leaving when I saw him, J.P., there in the back, hands in his pockets and dangerously handsome. I wished he hadn't seen me, unprepared for the moment, and gave myself a quick once-over – the corners of my lips, my eyes, under my nose, smoothed the eyebrows – before walking briskly over to him. Endearing wrinkles spread out from the corner of his eyes like fans, and a lone crease appeared on his left cheek. The charcoal-grey suit he was wearing was immaculate. George Clooney couldn't have held a candle to him.

"Hi! I didn't know you were coming," I said.

"I thought I'd drop by."

"The family's pretty special, isn't it?"

"Like Claudine."

"True."

Claudine is as special as I am boring. Two women on opposite ends of the spectrum, both left by their husbands.

"Right, I should say hello to her before I leave," he said.

"Do you have time for a quick sandwich?"

"Sure, why not?"

We made our way over to the buffet, likely organized by the Society of Local Farmers. There were the traditional sculpted mountains of coleslaw and potato and macaroni salad; little skewers of marinated onions, olives, and sweet pickles; devilled eggs; crudités and dip (a clever mix of ketchup and mayonnaise); and little triangles of crustless white and brown bread sandwiches. I took whatever was within reach, too busy trying to appear comfortable in my own skin to see where I was putting my hand. *Cretons*: not a good day. There's no elegant way to eat pork spread, period. J.P. contented himself with a piece of celery and two or three carrot sticks. Claudine and her daughters came over to join us.

"If it isn't the handsome J.P.!"

"I'm sorry for your loss, Claudine."

"It's sweet of you to stop by."

He leaned in to kiss her, seizing her arms like you see on the cover of a Harlequin novel. Then he extended a hand toward Laurie, who, smitten, looked up at him with big, beautiful eyes.

"I'm a colleague of your mother's," said J.P. "I'm sorry for your loss."

"Thank you. It was so nice of you to come."

He repeated the routine with Adèle, who offered him a limp handshake she did not bother to close. Merely breathing consumed all her energy, could he blame her?

"Come with us, Diane, we're going out for sushi."

"You're not staying longer with your family?"

"I already talked to my mother and sister. And the others . . . Are you eating cretons?"

"Uh . . . yeah."

"Throw it away. Come on, let's get out of here."

"Are you serious?"

"I don't feel like dealing with the microphone business. I told them to take the money out of Dad's account."

"Ladies, I think I'll head out now, my family's at home waiting. *Courage*, Claudine. And you too, girls."

I felt a knot in my stomach. No one was waiting for me at home, only a few plants I was cruelly neglecting. I who had once been so busy, who'd been so needed not that long ago, no longer knew what to do with myself. Life's a bitch. We should be able to recalibrate the hours in order to level the peaks and fill in the ditches.

"Till the next time, my darling J.P."

I wasn't able to enjoy the goodbye kiss he gave me; I was too focused on holding in my pungent pork breath. Such insignificant details often ruin the best moments in our lives. I'd once seen a bride burst into tears minutes before the official family photograph because she'd broken a nail.

J.P. turned to walk away. He was so handsome, even from behind. I've always had a thing for men's necks.

We ate sushi, drank sake, and laughed like crazy. Adèle even lifted her head several times to participate in the conversation. It was the first time Claudine had heard of Laurie having a boyfriend, and she was visibly touched. Death takes the place of shock therapy, sometimes.

And then Claudine wept. Finally.

13

In which I feed my
ex-mother-in-law a line

B LANCHE WANTED TO MEET up for a "serious discussion, woman to woman." I'd rather have had a tooth pulled without anaesthetic over putting up with one of her lectures, but I knew I had to deal with the infection before it spread. So, once it stopped raining, I dried off two deck chairs.

My mother-in-law didn't show up in loungewear and probably didn't even know the stuff existed. Instead she insisted we sit inside because what we needed to discuss was too delicate a matter to be in range of my neighbours' prying ears. In her mind, our tiny, 7,000-square-foot backyard just wasn't private enough. I hadn't bothered to remove the toilet paper and tissues from the bathrooms: Blanche doesn't use the toilet. In fact, it's always her I think of whenever men claim girls don't poop.

"Can I make you some herbal tea? Coffee? Would you like a glass of wine?"

"A canary would be lovely, darling."

Ordinary people would just ask for hot water with lemon.

She took off her cashmere shawl, examined the chair before sitting down, and then lowered herself with class, knees together, elbows in (obviously), and hands folded on the table. Everything with her was deliberate and, down to the smallest detail, calculated to provide an impression of both ease and humility. But it didn't work on me. I knew that a regular family of four could feed themselves for several months for the price of her most unassuming pair of earrings. Clearly, she'd decided on a pair of elegant pumps to be sure of seeing eye to eye. She'd always been thrown by my height.

"How are you doing, my dear?"

"I'm fine, thanks. And you?"

"I'm well, thank you. Despite this business of the separation . . ."

"Separation?"

"Yours."

"Yes. Sorry about that."

"It'll work out. Take one day at a time."

"Charlene is just adorable, you'll see."

"I'm sure she is. And since I've already spoken to Jacques several times about your little disagreement, I thought it was time for the two of us to have a little heart to heart."

"About . . . ?"

"Well. I know these things are very delicate, and you'll forgive me for being too forward, but a divorce would create waves and repercussions that wouldn't benefit anyone."

"We haven't talked about getting divorced yet."

"Exactly. I don't think your marriage is beyond saving."

"Jacques was the one who left. For another woman. It was a unilateral decision."

"Well, there you have it. Jacques's happiness is exactly what I wanted to discuss."

"Charlene's the one to ask about that now."

"It's yours I'm talking about, yours and Jacques's, your happiness that has . . . it seems to me, lost a little of the spark over the years. Look, I understand. I've been with the same man for fifty years. I know what it's like. I understand you perfectly."

I don't give a rat's ass.

"You can appreciate this isn't a subject one addresses with one's son. These things are best kept between women."

Jesus, she wants to talk about my sex life . . .

"I was wondering if you'd tried to shake things up, if you've tried therapy, if . . ."

"Hang on! Wait a minute! What are we talking about, here?"

"Jacques's happiness. And your own, darling, absolutely."

I'm not your darling.

"What do you mean by 'happiness'?"

"What with Jacques explaining to me he was no longer happy – which is the reason he left – I wondered if you had stopped . . . how should I put this . . . satisfying your husband?"

Christ!

Evidently she believed that I'd driven Jacques out of our conjugal bed because I wasn't fucking him enough, fucking him badly, or not sufficiently "shaking things up." And my minx of an ex-mother-in-law believed she had the right to hold me accountable for my sexual services because the honour and fortune of the family empire would suffer from our divorce. The "repercussions" she alluded to were obviously nagging at her. She didn't give a shit about our happiness, she even pronounced the word like others coughed up phlegm.

I could have thrown my hot water – mug and all – in her face, but she would have sued me for assault and loss of enjoyment of life. I couldn't lay a hand on her, not even a fingertip, or she'd have found a way to twist my actions into a form of aggression.

So I went with the sneakiest method, which was also the cruellest. It was so easy, I even felt a little bad after she left. I annihilated her, and she supplied the poison.

"Look, it's embarrassing to have to tell you this."

"Just think of me as an old friend who only wants the best for the family – your family."

"It's just that over the past few years, Jacques was starting to get . . . more . . . well . . . demanding."

"Demanding?"

"Yes. I wasn't able to . . . I don't know how to put this . . . fulfil his . . ."

"Fantasies?"

"That's right, his fantasies."

"But everyone has fantasies, darling. It's normal."

"Maybe. But with Jacques, they'd . . . well . . . they'd taken on a new character."

"What do you mean, 'new character'? Did he ask to role-play?"

"Umm . . . I suppose. He liked scenarios that made me really uncomfortable."

"Oh? Wasn't there a way to compromise?"

"Uh . . . no. But I don't think I should tell you about it."

"Is it really so bad?"

"Yes."

"Oh, come now. You're scaring me."

. . .

I was having fun retelling my story. Claudine was at the edge of her seat.

"Oh, come on, what did you say that was so awful?"

"Think about it, what would really kill her . . ."

"You've got me."

"I told her Jacques wanted me to dress as a guy so he could get it up."

"Oh God, you didn't!"

"Yes, ma'am!"

"What did she say?"

"Nothing. She covered her mouth with her hand to muffle a little squeak, picked up her things, and rushed out. I just sat there and finished my hot water with lemon."

"So now she must think . . ."

". . . the gay gene is her doing! Screw her!"

"I bet she'll ask Jacques if it's true."

"Never in her life. We were talking 'woman to woman.' She'd never involve him."

"Well, too bad for her, the old witch!"

When we'd announced, a few years back, that Alexandre was bringing his boyfriend to the family Christmas party, there'd been quite a stir. (We'd expected as much, hence the pre-emptive announcement to the so-called family.) Since, according to Blanche's genealogical research, both the Valois and Garrigues lines included only "normal people" – no branches of the family tree had dried up so far – the possibility that the "flaw" might have come from my side was mentioned. Jacques had clenched his teeth and tightened his fists in an effort to defend his son and "everybody like him," but the nasty exchange of words only escalated, forcing us to revise our holiday plans that year. World views had collided in an intergenerational Big Bang with a lot of collateral damage. To my mother-in-law, homosexuality was a disease with an as yet undetermined cause, like allergies. And, confronted with such narrow-mindedness, I got a little carried away and used words in tune with my feelings. I called her a "demented old bigot," among other things. Even today, some of the wounds are still open and festering. Our relationship has not been the same since, like one of those reconstituted vases that fool no one, their fault lines still visible and the whole structure compromised.

I was never out to avenge myself, but that day my ex-mother-in-law handed me the opportunity on a silver platter. And I took it. I still resented her, that I'll admit, and just picturing her torture herself over how she might have engendered what she'd imagine to be such an aberration gave me a delicious sense of satisfaction.

In all honesty, we'd wound up utterly bored in bed, Jacques and I. We were stuck on autopilot, doing the same things in the same order, over and over. No, we certainly hadn't managed to shake things up. At its core, our life had ended up taking on a time-worn patina. Proposing anything new would have been to acknowledge the ennui neither of us was ready to address. And even if I'd had the guts to suggest something new, I'd have been terrified of his judgement, just as I'd have feared his suggestions if he'd dared to make any. We were prisoners of the centrifugal force of our relationship pushing us inexorably apart.

Whenever he did want to have sex, Jacques would say, "Wait for me, I'm coming!" as soon as he saw me getting ready for bed. I'm boring – I have always been – and the only thing I want to do at the end of the day is sleep. While I'd made the effort to prioritize other things over sleep in those first years of marriage, it's true that for some time I'd gladly given myself over to the sandman anytime the opportunity arose. I used sleep like others did migraines. I loved my husband with all my heart, but my body was telling me – commanding me – to sleep, and there was nothing I could do about it. Plus, I knew Jacques was too respectful to ever wake me up to satisfy him.

Not all women are so lucky, office gossip has taught me.

So no, we never shook things up in bed, neither with him cross-dressing or me in a schoolgirl outfit. We treated our desire like a hygienic matter, like a necessary routine. It was no surprise, then, that my rhythmically challenged husband eventually sought "happiness" elsewhere.

But absolutely none of this was my ex-mother-in-law's business. That she believed she had a right to know the details of my sex life infuriated me. As soon as she stepped out the door, I went to grab the sledgehammer.

Once I'd calmed down, I read Antoine's text: "Love you, Mum."

14

In which I say "yes" one more time

"So you think Jacques is going to come back?"

"I don't know, I was just talking."

"It's a serious question: are you expecting Jacques to walk back through the door?"

The mandarin collar jacket she was wearing gave her a stern look. She was swinging a fountain pen back and forth between her fingers like a metronome, to the beat of my confessions. Maybe she didn't like regular ballpoint pens; I never asked.

"Diane?"

"It's not an impossible turn of events. It happens a lot."

"So you're hoping he'll come back?"

"Honestly? Yes."

"Why?"

"Because it would be easier. I'm thinking of the kids, especially."

"But your kids are out of the house."

"Yes, but Charlotte is probably going to move back home, she only left for school. And who knows about the other two. Relationships don't last long these days. They might need a place to land at some point."

"But Jacques doesn't need to be there."

"It would be weird without their father around. They always saw us together, the house was *ours*. I don't know . . ."

"You think your kids won't come home if Jacques isn't there?"

"They might not want to."

"Why is that?"

"I don't know."

"Did your parents split up?"

"When I was twenty."

"Were you still living at home?"

"No, I had an apartment."

"How did things go between them?"

"Pretty badly."

A raising of the eyebrows. "Tell me about that, Diane."

"My parents sold the house, and my mum found an apartment on the third floor of a beige building in a beige neighbourhood. My dad moved to Sherbrooke."

"So you stayed with your father or mother once you finished university?"

"I went to my mother's for a month. The saddest month of my life."

"Why do you say that?"

"It was just sad. It wasn't our house anymore, and I didn't like it. There were no memories, no neighbours, no friends, no back lane, and it didn't smell like home . . . When I got up at night I didn't know where I was, and when I saw the parking lot through the window, I just wanted to cry."

"And things were different in your own apartment?"

"No, that wasn't home either. I had roommates and knew it was only temporary. To be 'home' was to be at my mum's place, but I never felt comfortable there. I didn't even have a room. I slept on a pull-out in the living room, and she had the TV on all day to keep her company. She was so happy to be there! 'Much less work, much less to clean.' But for me, it was sad. Just sad."

"Hmm. And what if he never comes back?"

The possibility was so fabulously difficult to picture that I was still avoiding it.

"I know I should think about it, but I can't. I just can't."

"And what would you do if he did come back?"

"*Oh boy* . . . I don't know. He'd have to buy me a new ring for a start – a hell of a big one!"

"How big?"

"As big as the mess he's made."

"And you'd be able to forgive him?"

I'd asked myself the question a million times. The road to my forgiveness would be long and winding; he would need to redeem himself big-time. I wanted him to suffer, for him to blame himself, for him to crawl, beg, plead, and break down at my feet.

"Maybe."

"Do you still love him?" I couldn't bring myself to answer her question.

"Diane?"

"Yes."

15

In which I take a dislike to leaf blowers

THE OPPORTUNITIES FOR VENGEANCE afforded by Charlene and Blanche should have appeased me; instead, they raised the hackles of an acute irritability that, surprisingly, I had never encountered in myself. Not yet, at any rate. Whether my anger had always been there, lying dormant, or had suddenly flourished into being because Jacques had left was immaterial and had the same result: I ended up destroying something.

Jacques had often reproached me, saying I didn't know how to relax. And he was absolutely right – I didn't. It was a bad habit I'd developed raising children and working full-time. Even after the kids moved out, and despite the hours of freedom that subsequently fell down upon me like manna, I never managed to change pace. I still ate breakfast standing up at the corner of the counter and scheduled hair appointments in between running errands, housecleaning, paperwork, organizing birthday parties, and helping with this and that. All my free time evaporated in the zeal of my rushing about to get everything done, as if I was afraid of the void. I was continually in awe of my colleagues discussing the books they'd read or the movies they'd watched over the weekend.

So now – as much to prove to myself that I could as to calm the rage within me – I decided to relax. I was willing to do anything, to live in filth or eat frozen TV dinners, if that's what it took. I would master the art of doing nothing, and let it cost what it cost. I'd already reclaimed my Wednesday nights.

Thursday night

I had to comb through the entire Murdoch file to see where the order to the wholesaler had gone wrong. Normally, I'd have stayed at work and thrown myself into the task until death ensued. But that night I decided to go home, order a takeout box of chicken and finish every last French fry out on the back deck without a single regret. I did nothing but savour what I brought to my mouth. Between gulps of the Château Margaux I'd taken up from the cellar, still filled with decent bottles of wine, I licked my salty, sauce-covered fingers. Yes, it's true: a sacrilege. The only shadow cast over the scene? Mr. Nadaud had chosen the moment to mow his lawn and tend to the hedges. He'd been retired for a while and could have picked any time of day – when the rest of the neighbourhood was at work, for instance – but suddenly he'd felt the need to "spruce things up" in my company.

After scraping the bottom of the container clean – I'd have licked it if I'd been unobserved – I went back inside and planted myself down in front of the TV, slumping into my papasan chair like a lazy teenager. (I still hadn't replaced the couch.) I knew exactly what to do as each of my children had been through this phase – Antoine never really grew out of it.

As the wine worked its magic, I entertained myself watching a dumb spy movie in which all the bad guys were ugly and all the good guys were attractive. And even though their guns were smaller, they wreaked much more havoc than the bad guys. *The best things come in small packages.*

Friday morning

I made a point of getting to work a few minutes late, just to honour my new resolution. Claudine was waiting for me, bouncing up and down excitedly and clapping her hands.

"Go look! There's a surprise on your desk!"

"What for?"

"It's not from me!"

"Who's it from, then?"

"Josée."

"Josée who?"

"J.P.'s secretary!"

"Josy?"

"Her real name is *Josée*."

"You're kidding me."

"I've got her personnel file."

"I like Josée better."

"Who cares? Quick, open it!"

I had barely any time to feel butterflies in my stomach before I was pulling out my wonderfully heavy blue boots. There was a bottle of wine in each – actually, one of sparkling wine and another of white – along with a little card that I quickly slipped into my pocket.

"Are those the boots you gave J.P. the other day?"

"Yeah, they're my boots. My new old pair. Resoled."

"With some nice bubbly!"

"You should come over and drink it with me."

"When?"

"Whenever you want."

"I've got the girls until Sunday afternoon."

"Sunday evening, then. Perfect! I'll put it in the fridge."

"So, are you going to read the card now or Sunday?"

"What card?"

Because it was crazy, given the work I needed to finish, I decided to take the afternoon off and enjoy the beautiful day. I was going to drag the papasan out onto the deck, wrap myself in an alpaca throw, curl up into a ball inside it, and soak up the sun while reading a little and watching the leaves fall. I'd been given some two dozen novels from my kids over the years, none of which I'd ever found time to start. My brain needed exercise. Probably more than my body did, which was saying a lot. I ended up falling asleep. The Nadauds' lawn still smelled like freshly mown grass.

Friday afternoon

I could feel the heat radiating off J.P.'s card, tucked into the right-side back pocket of my jeans. It was unlikely to contain any earth-shattering revelations, though possibly a few sweet words. I put off reading it to make the giddiness last, basking in the feeling before I dove in. Meanwhile, Mr. Michaud had taken out his electric sander and begun working on his beloved deck. I thought he'd given it a complete overhaul at the beginning of the summer, but maybe I'd gotten the houses mixed up. At least he was going at it in the middle of the afternoon on a workday. I couldn't complain. Heavy machines were already roaring to life at and around number 5412 just down the street, which had recently sold. I had no idea what the new owners were planning, but teams of workers had been on the job by 7 a.m. every day for weeks now. The *tak-tak-tak!* of the nail guns had rocked my post-bombshell catalepsy.

I resisted the pull of the card in my pocket for another hour before opening it. Almost an hour. Okay, a few minutes.

"Shit!"

His chicken-scratch handwriting made me go back in to get my glasses. It was the first time I'd received a card from a man other than Jacques – even at that, I couldn't remember the last one he'd given me – and my eyes had become too old and tired to read without help.

Drum roll, please. The opening of the card.

The boots look too good on you. And you have really beautiful eyes. Cheers!
JP

Things between us would never go any further but, at that moment, the simple compliment made my heart skip a beat. Everything slipped away, even the noise of the sander and jackhammers. I had "really beautiful eyes" and that was enough. I had been reborn and all it had taken was a compliment. The only snag: I couldn't stop wondering if Jacques and Charlene's story had started the same way. I would need to go through Jacques's most recent gifts.

Friday night

It was the cold that woke me. The cold and the sound of a lawn mower belonging to Mr. Gomez, my neighbour on the left. But I couldn't be angry with him since he'd spent the past few months helping me with the furniture I'd "moved" out of the window and onto the curb, no questions asked. His wife kept an eye on what was happening through her kitchen window, too. They'd probably known before I did that my marriage was falling apart. I'm sure I'd have learned a bunch of things if I'd just asked the neighbours.

I retreated inside.

There was a voicemail from Jacques. He wanted me to send a text letting him know a good time to call. He said he didn't want me to call him, for obvious reasons. So of course I called him. Once, twice, three times, ten times, until he picked up.

"Diane, I'd rather we talked when it's a good time for both of us."

"Nothing serious, I hope."

Seriously, he could have broken both legs and I wouldn't have batted an eye. I caught myself hoping he'd at least caught the flu, a little pneumonia, or a nasty case of foot fungus. Even better, warts. Hundreds of warts.

"No, nothing serious. But now's not a good time. Can I call you back tomorrow?"

"No, I won't be around."

"I can't call your cell?"

"Uh . . . there's no signal where I'm going."

"Oh? There are still places with no reception?"

He was annoyed. I could tell by his sarcastic tone.

"Just say whatever it is you wanted to say and we'll be done."

"We have people here for dinner. I'd rather call you back."

Of course: Friday night, the weekend, friends, good wine, lots of fun, and a little steamy sex after dessert. The bile in my stomach rose all the way to my gums. What people, anyway? His colleagues, our friends, our children? New friends in their early thirties?

"I'll call you when I get back," I said.

"When will that be?"

"When I get back."

"I'd like to set a date."

"Okay. The twenty-third."

"The twenty-third?"

"What's today's date?"

"The third."

"Perfect. The twenty-third."

"That's three weeks away! You'll be gone for three weeks?"

"Yes."

"Where?"

"Somewhere with no reception. Okay, I'll let you go."

And I hung up. I'd already demolished the kitchen buffet my ex-mother-in-law had given us. And if I had a go at the table, I wouldn't be able to have "people" over for dinner. I reread J.P.'s card to try to pull myself together.

"You've got beautiful eyes, Diane. Beautiful eyes, and nice boots."

I went back outside for a breath of air. Mr. Nadaud was using his blower to chase three or four leaves that had the audacity to settle in his yard. There are by-laws for watering the grass; there should be some for leaf-blowing, too. Rakes are always better, anyway, since they let you gather the leaves together and actually pick them up rather than blow them into the street or onto your neighbours' property. I slipped into my blue boots and went for a walk. Even though I'd been pruning back my surfeit of furniture for months, I continued to suffocate in a house bursting with happy memories that were making me miserable.

I hadn't walked around the neighbourhood in a long time. I'd gotten out of the habit after the kids had grown up. We'd taken to driving them around town, Jacques and I, until they learned how to use public transportation. Then they'd bought their own cars – except for Charlotte, who broke out in hives simply at the idea of owning a polluting engine – and everybody had gone off on their own, by which time I'd completely lost touch with my own neighbourhood. And I have a terrible confession to make: I can't walk for the sake of walking without a stroller or a plan. I've lost the ability to "stroll." Going nowhere is harder than it seems.

The little shoe repair shop at the corner of Rue des Lilas had shut down. I went over to peek inside: only empty shelves and wood crates resting on a thick layer of dust. A yellowed sign fixed to the door read "We sharpen skates," like a faithful soldier refusing to surrender despite the general rout. It was where we used to have our shoes resoled or holes added to our belts when contentment thickened our waists. I hardly ever wear a belt anymore – skirts hide my rolls better – and rarely wear my soles out anymore. My waist will attest to that.

Three blocks down, I came across the abandoned video store. The shelves were still stacked with old VHS boxes with faded covers. Way in the back, I could see the door to the adult section was wide open. Somehow we'd convinced the kids that going in there would make them blind – until Antoine slipped in one day when we weren't looking and came out shouting, "I saw a woman with boobs *this* big and somebody else was putting a penis in her mouth, and . . . !" Alexandre and Charlotte had covered their ears so they wouldn't go deaf.

I turned on the heels of my newly soled boots and went home before my walk turned into a despairing stroll down memory lane that would spoil my good mood. There was bound to be a decent movie on Netflix.

I stopped in front of 5412, now two and a half storeys high. It was 6:42 p.m. and the site was still buzzing with activity. I stood with my hands on my hips, to make it clear that I was hardly ecstatic about the glass cube being erected in front of me. A man in a construction helmet and work boots approached me. Like all men who end up embracing mainstream fashion by claiming to flout it, his beard was too bushy and a few bizarre patterns were tattooed on his arms. Strange, isn't it, how tattooed men are always hotter than everyone else and wear short sleeves more often. A toothpick bobbed up and down in the corner of his mouth as he spoke.

"Evening, miss!"

We were off to a good start: I wasn't a "little lady" and he was attractive.

"Hello."

"Can I help you?"

"Yes, certainly. You can tell me what it is you're doing."

"Uh . . . we're building a house."

"Oh! I'm glad we sorted that out. Here I was thinking it was an aquarium you were building."

"You live in the neighbourhood?"

"Yes. I'm at 5420, two houses over."

"You're in the old Cape Cod?"

"That's me."

"Nice neighbourhood."

"It is, actually. How long until you're done here?"

"If we work evenings, we should finish up in four to six weeks. We've got to be out by mid-October at the latest."

"What do you mean by 'evenings'?"

"By law, we're allowed to keep working until 7 p.m."

"Every day?"

"No, we stop at 5 on Saturday and Sunday."

"Weekends too?"

"You bet! It's a big job. I've got two full teams going."

"How early do you start on weekends?"

He looked away and cleared his throat.

"Seven."

"Seven in the *morning*?"

"I don't have a choice."

"I don't care! This is a residential neighbourhood! People live here!"

"I know, ma'am."

"What's the big rush? What happens if you don't finish by mid-October?"

"The client won't be happy."

"The client? And what about us, his neighbours? He's willing to piss everyone off for weeks just so he can move in on time? Is he sleeping on the streets, your millionaire?"

"I'm sorry, miss, but that's what the contract stipulates. We had a few problems, late deliveries, things like that."

"Well, of course, it always takes more time than you think!"

"He's within his rights. We're abiding by the law."

"His rights, my ass! I've had enough of this 'my rights' business. Rights come with a little respect!"

"To be completely honest, I'd be happy to go home and knock back a beer right about now."

He took out his toothpick and shrugged his shoulders as if the matter were out of his hands. The fireball and three-headed dragon adorning his arm grew a bit with the effort of the muscle. In about thirty years, the tattoos would droop in a mess of faded ink on wrinkled flesh. The dragon would look like a handful of shrimp.

"You tell your client the neighbourhood's had it with all these bullshit renovations. And if he doesn't show up on my doorstep with an apple pie the day he moves in, he risks me coming by with a sledgehammer! Let him wipe his ass on the damn pie!"

"Noted, miss."

I turned back to the sidewalk and headed toward my beautiful Cape Cod style house, built when the neighbourhood was still just an open field. Back then, the construction crew could have worked all night and no one would have complained. A few animals, maybe.

Sprinklers spat bursts of water onto the Nadauds' verdant lawn. So much water and electricity to keep a small patch of land alive, one that would be struggling soon enough under several feet of snow and ice. To what end? If the myth of Sisyphus had not existed, I'd have invented it just for him.

Back in the kitchen, I took a crowbar and ripped out the speakers screwed into the wall, then pitched them outside through the open window. I put on a Florence K album and settled back into the papasan chair with a glass of Aligoté to admire the weeds growing unrestricted in my yard. Amid the tall reeds swaying in the breeze, small wildflowers with tousled heads were defiantly blooming. Had I known my unkempt garden would be so beautiful, I'd have cancelled my landscaper's contract a long time ago.

From the roof of number 5412, where three men were unloading shingles and other supplies, the hipster I'd spoken to earlier waved at me. Great. If they were adding a roof deck to my neighbour's aquarium, I'd be kissing my privacy goodbye.

Saturday morning

I went outside with my bowl of café au lait, without the lait – I'd forgotten to pick some up, again. Mr. Nadaud approached me hesitantly, throwing a few glances back at his kitchen curtains that were swaying like seaweed. It was one of two things: either he wanted to apologize for making so much noise in general, or he was coming to complain about the music I'd played last night until nine. Which was how long it took me to finish the bottle of wine.

"Hello!"

"Good morning!"

"How's it going, Mrs. Valois?"

"Fine. And you?"

"Eh, my knees are starting to give me trouble, but other than that . . ."

"You wouldn't know it, watching you work as you do!"

"Work keeps a man young."

"And how's your wife doing?"

"Marvellously, thanks. She says hi." I waved in the general direction of the windows, not sure which one offered the best view of us.

"To what do I owe the pleasure?"

"Well, it's . . . uh, I don't meant to be rude . . ."

"Is it about the music yesterday?"

"No! No, no problem there. We couldn't hear it inside anyway. And it's your right."

"Well, I'm glad. I thought I'd bothered you."

"It's actually about the lawn."

"The lawn? But your lawn is gorgeous! It's so thick it almost looks fake."

"Thanks, that's nice of you. But I meant yours, actually."

"Mine? Hah! You mean my hayfield?"

"That's right."

"I think it's pretty. Feels like we're in the countryside, don't you think?"

"Uh . . . I . . . I wanted to offer to mow it for you. I have the equipment."

I honestly hadn't noticed. He had so much gear his car no longer fit inside the garage.

"Mow it?"

"Yes, as a favour to a neighbour."

"That's nice of you, thanks."

"My pleasure."

"But I like it the way it is for the moment."

"Oh. Well, uh . . ."

"Is it bothering you?"

"Uh . . . well . . . uh . . . yes."

"Why?"

"Because of the weeds crossing over. The wind's blowing pollen and seeds into our yard."

"But you don't have a single weed on your lawn!"

"No, because I work really hard to keep them out. But it's tough, being next to a wild field. The weeds take root and spread underground . . ."

"I'm sorry, but it's a question of taste. You like grass, I like hay."

"I understand that, but your preference affects ours, if you see what I mean."

"Sure, maybe, but then again yours affects my quality of life."

"Your quality of life?"

"Yes. All the mowing, the Weed-Eater, the sprinklers, the leaf blower, not to mention the pesticide poisoning . . ."

"I don't have a choice with all that hay!"

He seemed devastated but there was no way I was going to let him cut my hay. His wife, the shadow behind the curtain, must have seen – what with his defeated expression – that he'd come back empty-handed. I'll admit, I was being difficult on purpose and could easily have cut him a deal: mow the lawn if it pleases you, but the machines only come out between 8 a.m. and 6 p.m. on weekdays. That would have given him a good fifty-hour window each week to primp his grassy carpet – which the little signs he planted every ten feet declared it was forbidden to walk on.

Halfway between our two decks, he turned around.

"Umm . . . excuse me for asking, Mrs. Valois, but do you think you'll keep the house, or do you plan to sell it?"

"Delaunais! My name is Diane *Delaunais*!"

Saturday afternoon

Charlotte met me at the park for my third jogging lesson. Her patience, her kindness, never ceased to amaze me. Maybe there'd been a mix-up at the hospital when she was born.

"Today, we'll alternate between walking and running, but the breaks won't be as long."

"I'll follow your lead, sweetheart."

We must have seemed a predictable pair: the wealthy older woman and her pretty young trainer. In reality, I was what the trainer would become twenty-five years and thirty-five pounds later. My budding double chin was simply a future projection of her own, still hewn in firm features defying the pull of gravity. In the moment, I found myself as ugly as she was beautiful, which was curiously reassuring.

I sweated blood and water for twenty minutes before giving up. I couldn't help it. I don't like suffering in any form. I never did, and don't wish it on anyone. Well, almost anyone. (In this chapter of my life, I was like everybody else and believed a certain amount of suffering to be deserved.) We walked back to the house arm in arm, ignoring the sweat or anything else that might have offended strangers.

Once Charlotte was inside, she was quick to criticize my latest remodelling efforts.

"Mum!"

"Yeah?"

"Where did the buffet table go?"

"The buffet table?"

"Yes, Grandma's beautiful maple sideboard?"

"It was too big. I wanted to declutter."

"Oh my God, you've got to stop! I would have taken it."

"Come on, where would you have put it in that tiny apartment? Your roommates wouldn't have been happy."

"Mum . . ."

"I was a little irritated by Grandma's visit the other day. And this was the result."

"You ripped out the speakers!"

"Because I wanted to listen to some music outside. It's impossible to relax when your neighbours are hyper-obsessed with cutting their grass."

"So you had to rip them out?"

"Yes."

She sighed softly, holding back the urge to lecture me.

"Don't tell your brothers, okay?"

"They'll notice things are missing everywhere. And they'll see the holes."

"Maybe we could have dinner together next Saturday?"

"Saturday? Sure, that works for me."

"We can go apple picking in the afternoon and then bake an apple crisp. And I'll make a stew."

"Vegetarian?"

"I'll make two."

"Yesss!"

"We can pretend it's Thanksgiving."

"But the boys won't come apple picking, you know what they're like."

"That's fine. The two of us can fill a basket by ourselves, and that'll be enough."

Saturday night

I made myself an *omelette natural*. It's such a lame meal for a Saturday night that it sounds better if you say it in Spanish. And since I had no idea what wine to pair with plain old eggs, I fell back on a perfectly adequate herbal tea. Then I went through every room in the house, treading as lightly as I could so as not to disturb anything – not even the dust I'd stopped sweeping up. But now memories were rising out of the cracks of the floorboards, merciless as blackflies.

Night-time, Jacques pacing the hallways and whispering nursery rhymes to Alexandre, who is determined not to sleep. *This kid is going to drive us crazy.*

Jacques shaving in the bathroom next to Antoine, who is scraping shaving cream off his cheeks with a plastic spoon as he listens to his father explain that you need facial hair to use a razor.

Me bringing grilled cheese sandwiches to the boys, busy building a Lego super-structure on the floor of their room with their dad, still in pyjamas. It's a Saturday, they can have lunch wherever they want.

Jacques is struggling with an elastic band as he tries to gather Charlotte's hair in a ponytail. I hide, so I can laugh and not be seen. When she screams, I see that he's missed a few strands on top.

The wind roaring as we make love headily, our gasps merging with the wind's gusts.

Jacques putting a warm blanket over my shoulders as he kisses me on the forehead. I close my eyes, savouring the touch of his hand as it grazes my arm. We spend long nights watching over the kids as a stomach flu makes the rounds. When it's our turn, we have nothing left to vomit up.

Jacques cradling Alex in his arms, eyes closed as if in prayer. We'd feared the worst when he tumbled down the stairs like a rag doll. Alex dreads escalators to this day.

Jacques rubbing his ashen temples in front of the bathroom mirror: the bags under his eyes reflect the size of his workload.

Me crying in Charlotte's bedroom because it's time for her to move out, and I'm in her room sobbing. Jacques comes and sits down on the bed next to me, sighing heavily. It's always been his way of crying. He puts his hand over mine. I had no way of knowing, then, that my time with him was soon to run out.

Me washing the kids' sheets, even when they're not dirty. I want their beds to smell like vanilla if ever they show up without warning. Jacques says, "Honestly, Diane."

Me entering our deserted bedroom. I've transferred all my belongings to the chest and closet in the guest room. But I haven't been careful enough and I find myself staring at my reflection in the full-length mirror on the other side of the door. I am a woman in tatters, lacerated by departures. As long as Jacques was still around, the seams held. But once he left, I disintegrated into particles of nothing. I loathe myself, body and soul. I'm totally alone. I don't know how to keep going.

"*Honestly, Diane.*"

Sunday afternoon

Claudine showed up earlier than expected. I was reading in my papasan, soothed by the cacophony of drilling.

"I rang the doorbell! You didn't hear it?"

"Well, no. It's a little noisy back here, surely you noticed."

"My God! Are Sundays not sacred in the suburbs anymore?"

"Wow, you look good!"

Her outfit screamed sexy-chic: black, with a gorgeous blue-grey jacket and vertiginous heels. She'd done her hair, her make-up, put on perfume, and looked super-cute.

"You didn't get dolled up like that just for me, I hope?"

"Just for you."

"You went over the top."

"You deserve it."

"The girls are with their dad?"

"Yup, and I can't say I'm sorry to be rid of them for a few days. I was about to murder one of them."

"I thought things were better."

"If I ignore the fact that school called about Adèle on Thursday, and Laurie gives me attitude anytime I ask her for something, then sure, everything's great. I think Laurie and her boyfriend broke up."

"Already?"

"Yes, already. Hey! Nice yard."

"I'm going for a country look."

"Less upkeep."

"And it's prettier, no?"

She dropped into one of the deck chairs that had luckily had time to dry.

"So, how about that bubbly?" she said.

"It's 3:30 in the afternoon!"

"The perfect time for bubbles."

So we opened the sparkling wine and started a session of office gossip. We spent a good hour lamenting the company's lack of organization, its incompetent staff, its secretaries dressed like porn stars, the air conditioning that never worked right, the fact that Chez Joe – our favourite snack bar – had closed; Jeanine's illness, how Suzette was fired, and on and on. Claudine took the opportunity to let me in on a few secrets about the personnel files still being processed by HR. I'm silent as the grave, and she knows it.

I'd never repeat anything she tells me – and I was astonished to find out that Martha's health problems were a front for a full tummy tuck and boob job. Seriously, it didn't show, a job well done. Claudine had noted the surgeon's contact information, just in case.

We were a little tipsy by the time she finally got down to business.

"Okay, I need to see J.P.'s card."

"Oh come on, it's nothing special."

"Yeah, right! Hand it over."

Claudine, a natural romantic, could read between the lines. In addition to my beautiful eyes, I also had nice legs – a compliment hidden behind the comment that my boots looked good on me – so he thought me pretty from head to toe and was probably secretly in love with me. Hence, said Claudine, the emphasis "you have *really* beautiful eyes." He'd proposed a toast to my "good health," which was an invitation, albeit indirect, to join him for a drink one of these days. All my attempts to dismiss the incident of the boots as insignificant were waved aside. We were talking destiny, a story inscribed in the Book of Love. The first page had been turned, and the ending was bound to be a happy one.

"Stop! Stop! It has nothing to do with fate, Claudine. You're the one who made me go see him with some bogus file as an excuse because he's the only man I might have wanted to kiss – *if* he wasn't married, *if* the attraction was mutual, if the timing was right, and all the other ifs I can't think of right now."

"Fate willed me to send you in there."

"Except that I was the one who said he was the only possibility in the place!"

"Fate willed me to ask and for you to say his name."

"Well, your fate's a married man."

"And since when has being married stopped anyone? I'm sure if we bothered to do some research, we'd learn that married men cheat on their partners more often than unmarried men do. One hundred percent of the women here today can confirm that."

"Speaking of which, Jacques called me Friday. It seemed important."

"No!"

"I told him I couldn't talk to him before the twenty- third."

"Why the twenty-third?"

"Just to bug him."

"Well done."

"I wonder what he wanted from me."

"Diane . . ."

"What?"

"I can smell the divorce papers from here."

"Oh. That hadn't even crossed my mind."

"Tramps like her always want to get married."

We let ourselves ride the tide of our venomous cynicism until the bottle ran out. And that's when Mr. Nadaud came out, fraught that dead leaves had begun to decompose on his goddamn lawn. He plugged in the leaf blower and got down to business.

So I very calmly got up, marched across my field and then his yard, grabbed the cord, and pulled with all my might. The brand new Black & Decker heaved a final sigh before rolling over, lifeless. Though not quite as theatrical, I'd achieved the same result as Laurie had at the funeral, the plug twisting in the air and sending off a rash of sparks before conceding defeat. There. All taken care of in under ten seconds. Now we could continue drinking and listen instead to the hay swaying in the breeze.

Claudine was clutching her stomach with both hands as she laughed uncontrollably, and Mr. Nadaud was giving me the evil eye. But that's all he could do: the man didn't have an ounce of malice in him.

"So, what were we saying?"

"You're crazy!"

"It's Laurie's fault. I'm impressionable, what can I say?"

The police never came, the wine was consumed, and Mr. Nadaud holed himself up with his wife to prepare the leaf blower's funeral. Worst-case scenario, he'd have his revenge by mowing my hayfield while I was not around. In a way, that suited me. Vermin love hiding out in wild grasses.

The sky was magnificent to behold, the late afternoon sun casting a red glow onto everything it touched.

The white wine was fabulous, the fruit and cheese delicious, the silence marvellous. Even the guys working on 5412 had started packing their things. Claudine plugged her phone into the stereo, and we sang along to familiar Madonna tunes in high-pitched screams. We were the superstars, the virgins, the material girls of a suburb that no longer existed.

"I danced to this song once. I took ballet-jazz classes, I wanted to be a professional dancer like Irene Cara in *Flashdance*."

"I used to love this song!"

"I knew the choreography by heart. Check this out." Claudine kicked off her heels and set about dancing like Irene, pretending I was one of the judges from the video. She hopped up and down, pointing her toes and punching the air, did a few jumps as she rolled her head and even tried a split that wasn't half bad. Without editing, it wasn't quite as impressive as the movie was, but there was no question she owned the moves. Time had slowed her down – and she was restrained by her elegant outfit – but the magic wasn't lost on me in the slightest.

I wanted to warn her when she started backing up a little overzealously, but too late: she tripped and went flying off the deck before I could even open my mouth.

Lying on the ground in a bed of flattened hay, Claudine held one arm and let out a torrent of expletives, in which certain objects of the church were overrepresented. Two of the workers from the site down the street came over to see if everything was all right. They'd been watching us from their perch. Tattoo Guy was there, of course. But one look at Claudine's face, wrought with pain, told me we'd be sobering up in a crowded waiting room instead of inviting the men over for a drink.

"Let me see. It's your forearm that hurts?"

With his dirty, chapped, cracked hands, Tattoo Guy lifted her arm delicately toward him, like he was handling a newborn. Kneeling beside her, the moment charged with tenderness, his savage beauty clashed with her elegance in the unlikely duo they formed.

"I can't move it . . . *aggghh* . . . fucking hell . . . it hurts too much."

"What about your fingers?"

"I can move them, but *aahh* . . . not very well . . ."

"Did you fall directly on your arm?"

"Obviously, you damn fool . . . *aaaghh* . . ."

"Well, me, I wouldn't take the chance. I'd go in for X-rays."

I was too drunk to drive, and so was Claudine. Our heads were useless and so were our arms.

"I'll call a taxi."

"I can take you to the hospital. I'm heading into town anyway," said Tattoo Guy.

"Diane, stay here, otherwise you'll waste your evening. It'll be a long, boring wait."

"Exactly. Long and boring – I'm coming!"

"Then bring the wine."

"It's all gone."

"Goddamn it!"

And that's how we ended up wedged together on the bench seat of a pick-up filled with tools, next to a good Samaritan who smelled of sweat and hard labour just enough to mask our alcohol-soaked breath. I saw, now, the image tattooed on his arm: what I'd thought were flames was actually a woman's hair roiling around her naked body. From what I could make out through his body hair, she appeared quite fit.

At the hospital, we regaled the nurse with stories from our evening. We even included the leaf blower episode to add a bit of colour. She had no idea who Irene Cara was, but she could picture the scene and wondered why it hadn't been me doing the dancing. I wasn't the one dressed up, after all.

"I've got no rhythm. I can't dance."

"Ah."

She let it go; no doubt she'd seen her fair share of oddballs.

"So, you twisted something?"

"No, I fell! A nasty fall."

"Okay, so you fell. From about what height?"

"How high is the deck, do you think?"

"I don't know, three or four feet?"

"What type of surface?"

"Where I fell from, or where I landed?"

"Where you landed."

"Hay."

"Hay?"

"Yeah. Thank goodness!"

"Did you fall over the railing?"

"There isn't one."

"That's too bad."

"You're telling me."

"Go take a seat. They'll call you into triage shortly."

An hour later, the triage nurse took Claudine's vital signs. Then she immobilized her arm with a splint. We were sent to join the battalion of sick and wounded in the waiting room, the lot of us fighting pain and boredom with muted soap operas and outdated magazines.

A woman came in on a stretcher, screaming. She was held down with straps and her head thrashed violently from side to side like an oscillating sprinkler on full blast. (I know a lot about sprinklers thanks to Mr. Nadaud.) I couldn't tell if the pain was external or internal. Everyone in the waiting room sighed: she was the priority. Pain makes us selfish.

"Dementia, maybe?"

"Could just be a bad stomach ache."

"An ulcer."

"Peritonitis."

"Kidney stones."

The woman in the seat next to us chimed in.

"Maybe she watched her boyfriend stab her kids to death."

We had nothing to add. The idea struck us with an unspeakable horror that paralyzed tongue and brain. I glanced in her direction to see just what was wrong with her, but it was impossible to know. As was the case with pretty well everyone in the waiting room. Instinctively, I inched closer to Claudine.

Later, much later – well after the last atom of white wine had dissolved into our bloodstreams – Claudine started talking. She was looking straight ahead, as if the anguish of the wait had prompted her to make some intimate confessions.

"I always dress up when I see Philippe. And since we had to talk about Adèle today, I knew he'd have time to really look at me."

"Are you serious?"

"Uh-huh."

Her eyes, the eyes of a beautiful, strong woman, filled with tears.

"Claudine, shit . . ."

"I knew you'd understand. Unfortunately."

So she was holding out hope, just as I was. Two pathetic women sobering up in a decrepit old hospital. We needed to get out of there.

"So it's been a while since you made out with someone, too."

"*Pfff.*"

And she began laughing hysterically, letting the tears wash away what remained of her mascara.

"Okay then, name a guy you'd make out with. Quick! Don't think about it."

"Whatever doctor comes by next."

"Man or woman?"

"Doesn't matter."

Hours later

"You did diving and ballet-jazz at the same time?"

"And figure skating, gymnastics, painting classes, violin . . ." added Claudine.

"Holy shit! And you don't do any of those things anymore?"

"No."

"Why not?"

"I wasn't good at any of it. I should have been reading Heidegger," she said, mournfully.

16

In which I spill coffee

J.P.'s SECRETARY WAS ALL fired up, raring to get the week started.

"Can I help you?"

"No, I just came by to say a quick hello. I'll come back later."

"He's in Toronto until Wednesday."

"Oh, okay. I'll come by Thursday then."

"He's going to check in at the end of the day. I'll tell him you stopped by. What's it concerning?"

None of your business, you damn busybody.

"It's concerning my saying hello, that's all."

"Then maybe just shoot him an email?"

I wouldn't tell you, even if I did.

"Okay, maybe."

"Let me know if you want me to pass anything along."

Middle finger.

"Thanks."

I was dizzy with hatred for this woman when my phone started vibrating. The private investigator I'd hired a few weeks back wanted to hand me documents from Phase One of the process. When we'd first met, he'd suggested we focus on the eighteen-month block before Jacques left, in order to anticipate the bad news and avoid jumping straight into the "shit storm." He loved using excrement metaphors and talked constantly of "that ass-wipe." When you spend your life sifting through everyone else's crap, that's probably inevitable.

I said I'd meet him at Café, a decent greasy spoon near the office known, as you'd expect from the name, for its excellent coffee. It was easy enough for me to slip away from the office to attend to "urgent business," and as I owed him the balance for Phase One (along with a little extra for his printing the documents, dinosaur that I am), he was quick to agree to meet.

Henri Deraîche arrived at 10:15 on the dot. I suspect he'd kept out of sight until the appointed time to uphold his reputation as a reliable and exacting professional. He'd been just as punctual for our first meeting, smiling and relaxed and worlds away from the stereotype of a drunk detective in a crumpled beige trench coat, and much more like that of a geek who could hack into any computer system. That first day his hair was greased back in a slick wave, but he'd forgotten to wipe the sleep from his eyes. With his 10X glasses, it wasn't a very good look.

I was hoping he'd hand me a folder with two or three sheets confirming in large print that Jacques was somehow innocent and absolving him of blame. But, given the affair,

I had to anticipate a few scathing revelations that, though hardly surprising, would nonetheless hurt me deeply. As it happened, the P.I. handed me an envelope containing documentation so thick I almost dropped it.

"This can't be for me."

"Are you Diane Delaunais?"

"Yes."

"We met on August 29 to discuss your research request, no? Your ex-husband is Jacques Valois, partner at the firm Brixton, Valois, and Associates?"

"Uh-huh."

"Then this is yours. Here's the bill with outstanding fees to be settled, including printing costs. You'll find a breakdown of the time and researches conducted at the beginning of the document."

"But I don't understand. Why's it so thick?"

"It's mostly the emails."

"Emails?"

"Yes. I've printed them in full."

"Emails about what?"

"I'll let you read them for yourself. Whenever you think is the appropriate time."

The envelope between us contained a record of Jacques's conversations with others, most likely women. If I opened it, their voices would grate in my head like nails on a chalkboard and shred to nothing the last eighteen months of my marriage. And this was just the first batch, an initial stab to the gut, but one that meant almost certain death. The business trips, the conferences, the rounds of golf and late meetings whirled past me in a dizzying carousel of images. The cesspit of lies and paltry daily scheming would surely be stains upon pages I would never find the strength to read.

I managed, robotically, to get out my chequebook and write an amount in numbers and letters, and then to sign my name, Diane Delaunais. I didn't want a receipt.

"For the second phase, we can focus on the most significant time periods . . . Mrs. Delaunais?"

I couldn't formulate a reply. "Ma'am?"

"Oh . . . I . . . no. I'll be in touch."

"I understand. Take some time to think about everything. You know how to reach me."

"Yes, thank you."

He started to walk away, then turned back to me. "I, uh . . . I don't know if this will help at all, but I've seen much worse."

"No, that doesn't help."

"I'm sorry."

He left without another word, leaving me alone with a packet that had enough poison in it to ruin my life – or the illusion I'd had of it, until then. Stacked an inch high, these neatly bundled papers were certain to cast a harsh light over events of the last year and a half, pulling me out of the blissful darkness of ignorance. I might never recover.

My break had been done for some time when the server came by to ask if I wanted anything else. I tried to smile back, but the attempt must have been pathetic, and he lowered his eyes and went to wipe down another table. He probably believed the detective was my lover and that he'd come to dump me.

I texted the secretary of my department to say I'd been held up, I'd be back as soon as possible. It was the first time I'd ever asked her to cover for me. She didn't ask why.

"All good. Take as much time as you need."

I took a gulp of cold coffee, and let my eyes wander around the room. At one of the tables in the back, right next to the tree growing there – I never understood how a live tree could grow inside the restaurant – I spotted Mr. Dutronc, director of the Exports department.

He was rarely in the office, his work demanding that he travel all over to set up business deals. Sales had tripled since I'd started at the company, owing to the tentacles it dispatched to the four corners of the planet; our payslips, on the other hand, amounted to the same as always. Most of the contact we had with upper management was limited to unbearable speeches we were forced to sit through over breakfast meetings intended to help us maintain our ISO rating, among other things. During these trimesterly meetings – *trimenstrually*, you could say, given how excruciating they were – I gorged on pastries to distract myself from the hollow words of our deep-pocketed execs.

Mr. Dutronc was speaking animatedly to a pretty young woman – too pretty and too young, actually – who I recognized. She was one of two new interns we'd met at the previous breakfast seminar. I forgot which department she was in, but remembered her name, Gabrielle, because that's what I would have named Charlotte had Jacques let me. The poor girl was no doubt having to endure the old man's habitual litany of commercial "exploits" – enough to make you shudder – as he dressed them up in a bunch of dubious metaphors. Clients, first and foremost, needed to be "seduced," "charmed," "sucked off," and otherwise led down the rosy path and brought dangerously close to the act itself, at which point it was easy to close the deal. But much as I found our own encounters pathetic, he was harmless as long as it was all talk. It was much more worrying to see him, clearly in a position of authority, trying his patter on a young, vulnerable girl.

Discreetly, I kept watching to garner a sense of what was going on. Gabrielle was nodding at everything, nervously twirling a strand of hair, frenetically looking at her phone, fiddling with her nails, her lips, the palm of her left hand, and the corner of the table. Clearly, she was uncomfortable. I wanted to offer her my hand and say, "Come on, sweetie, let's get out of here." Every fibre of my motherly being was sounding the alarm. If it were Charlotte backed up against the wall like that, I'd have gouged out the man's eyes.

Those were the thoughts running through my mind when I saw the pervert's gummy hand cover her pale fingers like a dark cloud. What with the way her arm tensed it was easy to see she wanted to get away from him. Sensing that she might actually manage to, he'd closed his other hand over hers in a vice-like grip, forcing her to look up at him.

I shot out of my chair. "Get your hands off her right now! Don't even try it, you old asshole, she's not into you. *You could be her grandfather!* You don't scare me, even with your cash and filthy lawyers. I filmed the whole thing, you're in the shit! Ever heard of social media? If I were you I'd be really worried because the second someone starts digging a little deeper they'll realize you're rotten to the bone. There are a ton of journalists who'd love to expose a rat's ass like you for what you really are – that's what sells papers these days, sad as it is. I bet you spent the past thirty years letting your hands go wherever they want. But listen up – this is how it's going to work from now on: don't you ever touch this girl again, or any other girl for that matter. No one gave you the right! If I ever hear you've crossed the line, I'll make your head spin – and that's not a metaphor. So you're going to walk out of here and tell all your little buddies with wandering fingers that the days when work was an open bar are *over*, dipshit. You got that? *Over!*"

I kept hitting the table with my index finger until it hurt. Every syllable, *bam!* Every exclamation point, *bam!* I didn't even stop when my fingernail broke.

"Ma'am?"

"Excuse me, ma'am?"

Oh no. Getting up, I'd overturned my chair and the syrupy contents of my coffee were spilling across the table and pouring over the edge. The people around me were doing one of two things: staring at me, or trying *not* to stare at me. Thankfully, before any of the words had actually escaped, a safety valve had triggered somewhere in my brain, suddenly blocking my outburst. Still. I might have murmured something, it's hard to know. In any case, I was used to looking like a madwoman.

The director had repatriated his hands all the same. He looked at me without actually seeing me, the nameless employee. I unclenched my teeth ever so slightly and walked out. Just another thing to feel ashamed of: my cowardice to actually speak out.

• • •

Back at the office, Lynne was waiting impatiently.

"Accounting called about the Murdoch file. It seemed pretty important."

"Oh, yes, it is. Thanks. I'll take care of it."

"The colour palette came in for the new desks, take a look. If you ask me, the beige is verging on pink and the burgundy's too dark."

I chose the goose-poop greenish yellow, the ugliest colour of them all: I felt like sticking it to my desk. Management must have had friends in furnishing companies, looking to rid themselves of desks that weren't selling, to even propose such hideous colours, pals who delivered bloated invoices for short elevator trips.

I walked into my office and collapsed in my chair.

Nerves had exhausted me, and suddenly my legs weren't responding. I was still holding the hefty envelope of shame in one trembling hand and had started to hate the detective who'd amassed it by digging through my life and Jacques's, for all his ill-concealed crimes. He was supposed to repair my honour, to have restored it to me intact by virtue of a few expeditious, well-formulated sentences judiciously dispersed in a reassuring report. But he'd poked around in what I didn't want to know. Pressing down on the envelope with the entire weight of my body, I measured it: one inch. I broke the seal to feel the paper stock. Standard thickness with no card cover, it was an inch of grief on ordinary, partially recycled paper. I shoved all of it back into the envelope.

Claudine had stayed home with her nice new cast on. The fracture didn't prevent her from working, but she was taking a bit of time off to recover from the emotional strain. I called to check in on her and told her I'd managed to ruin all that remained of my life in the space of a coffee break. What can I say? I might be boring, but I'm efficient.

17

In which I examine the envelope and eat apple pie

O<small>NCE HOME</small>, I <small>LEFT</small> the envelope in the car delib-erately. I wanted time to think about what would happen if I opened it. I needed to feel my way around the abyss before throwing myself in.

It was nearly midnight when I left the house in my bathrobe to retrieve it, terrified a thief might stumble across it and parade my cuckolded existence across social media. I still had no idea what the damn envelope even contained. And that's when I saw the Nadauds in their kitchen, bright as the day, eating, a good six hours later than most. Despite the cold and my being so inappropri-ately dressed, I stood in the driveway, watching them cut into their food with knife and fork. A couple of ordinary people eating in the middle of a bizarre scene. I needed to take a closer look, and I had the perfect excuse.

Mr. Nadaud came to the door.

"Good evening!"

"Good evening."

"I wanted to apologize for the leaf blower. I'll replace it, of course."

"No need, I fixed it up and it's good as new."

"Oh, good! But still, I'm sorry for going at it like a wild thing. I really lost it back there."

His wife had just appeared behind him. She was clutching the collar of her sweater as women of a certain age do when they're afraid of catching cold.

"Don't worry about it," she chimed in, "we know you've had it rough lately. It's no joke what you're going through, we understand."

"That's very kind of you."

"And please forgive him, too. He can get so annoying about the lawn. It's practically a disease. Me, I'd have done the same as you, Mrs. Valois – oh! I'm so sorry, you must be using your maiden name again."

"I never took my husband's name, actually. Mine is Delaunais, but it's not a big deal."

"Would you like to come in for a piece of apple pie? I just took it out of the oven."

And that's how I found myself in my pyjamas in the Nadauds' kitchen at 12:13 a.m., chatting about the weather and eating apple pie. It was like a scene out of a David Lynch movie. It wouldn't have surprised me if their cat had suddenly started talking.

"Forgot something in your car?"

"Yes, some papers."

"In a brown envelope? Ha ha! Sorry."

"Ha! I know what you're thinking. But no, it's not money. It's a top secret file."

"Best not to take chances, someone might steal it. Especially if it's top secret."

"Can I ask you a question? It's a little nosy."

"Go ahead."

"Do you always eat this late?"

They flashed each other a sheepish look, as if I'd asked something truly intimate – like whether or not they still shared a bed.

"We've been doing so for a while, now. After we retired, it just sort of happened."

"We didn't really notice at first."

"Since we no longer have any reason to get up early, we've been sleeping in later and later."

"And staying up later and later. Now that we can record TV shows, we watch practically everything that's on."

"Do you watch any of the American shows?"

"Oh yes! We're really into *Game of Thrones* these days."

"We're always trying to predict what's going to happen next."

"So our days sort of ended up flipped around."

"Kind of like teenagers."

"Maybe. We never had kids."

"And we started working when we were teenagers ourselves."

They looked at their hands, the floor, then back up to the table, as if their thoughts had to make the sign of the cross before they could be expressed.

"I needed a hysterectomy the year we were married."

"Oh! I'm so sorry."

"No worries. It was a long time ago."

The way the words came out, I could tell she'd uttered them so many times they'd lost all meaning.

"Sorry about the bathrobe, I know it's weird. I was already in bed when I remembered the . . . the envelope."

"Sorry about our weekday habits, they're pretty weird too."

Then I remembered the Nadauds had the strange habit of wearing matching clothes according to the day of the week. You could set your watch by them. Alexandre had pointed it out to me soon after they'd moved in some fifteen years ago. (They'd sold their property in the city and used the money to buy a quiet place to retire in the suburbs.) That day – that day and night – they were wearing their "Monday clothes": grey pants and a navy shirt. The tops and bottoms were always the same colour, but in different styles. Practical for laundry, if less so for fashion. What's more, the sizes were completely off, either they'd put on weight without realizing it or their clothes had shrunk in the dryer. That said, when it comes to an unlikely reconciliation between neighbours discussing a lost uterus in the middle of the night over slices of apple pie, clothes don't matter all that much.

"Actually, another reason I came over is to see if you'd still like to mow my lawn. It would be a big help. I'll pay, of course."

"Out of the question! It would be my pleasure, a neighbourly service."

It wasn't true. I'd been determined to stand my ground when it came to the lawn, but the apple pie we'd shared in a world of such abysmal loneliness had melted my obstinacy. Even though I hate the word, it's the one that suits: I *pitied* them. Their tedium, thick as tar, hindered their movements and their voices. Everything about them was dull and grey, from the small porcelain cat to the painting, hanging on a beige wall, of a birch on a dismal plain. A few years from now, someone would find them mummified in their kitchen, their matching weekday outfits hopelessly faded. And I'd given them so much trouble about the lawn!

I left, feeling strangely alive in the biting cold of the night. I even stopped for a moment as I crossed my overgrown field, closed my eyes, and pictured myself far away in space and time in the midst of a wild grassland. The heat my clothes had retained was leaving me, molecule by molecule. If I remained still, not fighting the wind, perhaps I'd disintegrate altogether, my bones sprinkling the ground in a snowy powder. Disappearing that way would be just fine. I'd be everywhere and nowhere at once, any efforts to find me both easy and difficult.

Over the next few days I hid the envelope in different places, imagining I'd stop thinking about it if I buried it deeper and deeper in the recesses of my house. After trying all the closets, the bottom of cupboards, the dryer, different mattresses, bookshelves and filing cabinets (pursuing this logic, the best place to hide a leaf is in a forest), I ended up finding the perfect place, possibly *too* perfect – the hole I'd "inadvertently" made in the living room wall when I'd smashed the couch apart. I rolled up the envelope and slipped it into the opening. On the other side it unfolded itself and fell a few feet down to land between two wall studs. It would be impossible for me to retrieve it without opening up the wall to the floor. And what with the kids coming over on Saturday, it wasn't the time to start renovating.

• • •

J.P. returned to the office on Thursday, as expected. Josée-Josy stood up when I came in.

"Hello, Diane!"

"Hello, Josée!"

A wrinkle of annoyance appeared between her overly made-up eyes. She wanted nothing to do with her real name, that much was obvious. I smiled as naturally as possible, feigning innocence. Two could play at her game.

"Is Jean-Paul back?"

"Yes, he is. But he's on the phone at the moment. You could come by later. Or would you like to wait?"

"No thanks."

J.P.'s handsome head appeared in the doorway just as I was turning around.

"Hello! You came to see me?"

"Only if you have a couple of minutes."

"Josy, can you take messages for the next few minutes?"

"Sure."

"Thanks."

Once we sat down, it struck me that sending him a note would have been better.

"Thank you for the bottles of wine. Really, it was too generous."

"I shouldn't have?"

"No, you shouldn't have."

"It was my pleasure. Really. Though I didn't know if you cared for wine."

"Oh, I do. I do. I shared both bottles with Claudine."

"Oh, right!"

"Very. We ended up in the hospital, actually."

"Really? Too smashed?"

"No, no. Well, yes, maybe a little, but it's a long story . . . do you know *Flashdance*?"

"As in 'What a Feeling'?"

"You know that song?"

"Of course!"

"But it's such a girly movie!"

"Exactly. I was really into girls back then, so I was really 'into' that movie."

"Smart guy."

"But why the hospital?"

"Claudine fell and fractured her arm."

He tilted his head up forty-five degrees and turned his palms upward, wordlessly demanding more explanation.

"Remember the dance where the girl jumps around all over the place?"

"Yes, of course! The girl who gets a bucket of water dumped on her and then does a pole dance . . ."

"Uh, yeah. But I mean the part in the gym, with all the judges."

"Sure, sure, I remember. The girl's all sweaty, she points at the judges . . ."

"Exactly! Remember the part when she backs up and does those little kicks?"

"Yeah . . ."

"Well, picture it happening on a deck with no railing."

He put his head in both hands before leaning back and letting out a big, guttural laugh. Air coursed through his body with a fabulous abandon. I could just imagine him sitting with the boys, beer in hand, playing cards or watching a hockey game. The sort of bon vivant you come across at Happy Hour, who doesn't seem to notice the girls devouring the very sight of him between peanuts. While he was laughing so cheerily, I stared at his pink lips until, in my head, we were inches from making out. I leaned over gently, my stomach on fire, my lips touching his as we tilted our heads softly in opposite directions, our tongues warm, wet, longing . . .

"Diane?"

"Uh . . . yes?"

"You okay?"

"Yes, yes, sorry. I'm just tired. We got back late from the hospital."

"Listen, I'm sorry to hear about Claudine."

"Don't be. That's what happens when you act like teenagers. We'll laugh about it one day."

"I suppose so."

"Come by and sign her cast when she gets back. It's her first one ever, and she's pretty excited. Only don't tell her I told you."

"Don't worry, I won't."

He stood up to see me out, like a real gentleman. As his right arm swung toward the door, his left hand naturally found my shoulder and for one long, beautiful second his body was enveloping mine. He wasn't wearing cologne. I wanted time to freeze so that I could stay longer, snuggled against him, and stopped in my tracks.

"Thank you for the card."

"I meant what I said. I wanted you to know."

I was breathing way too fast. I would need a paper bag if I didn't get out of there soon enough.

"Bye."

"See you, Diane."

When I reached the fourth floor, I did a quick sweep of the hallway: empty. I took off my shoes and ran all the way to my office. I even went back and forth a few times. I was starting to understand what Claudine meant when she'd talked about a rebound.

• • •

"You won't believe this," I said breathlessly to Claudine when we caught up later.

"Did you get into more trouble?"

"No, it's good news!"

"I'll be the judge of that."

"I went to see J.P., like you told me to do. I thanked him for the wine and the card . . ."

"You didn't tell him about our night, did you?"

"Well, not the whole thing. Just the bit about us having to go the hospital. I mean, with your cast and all . . ."

"What did you say happened?"

"Uh . . . I said –"

"No, you didn't –"

"– it was because you tripped."

"Doing what?"

"Uh . . . dancing."

"*Diane!* Everyone's going to make fun of me!"

"Oh come on, no one's going to find out."

"Hello, Houston, we have a problem! The whole thing will get out!"

"So what? It's no big deal," I said nervously.

"For you!"

"Are you mad?"

"I'd planned on saying I fell from a ladder while I was cleaning the gutters or something."

"That's so boring."

"Yeah, but breaking your neck because you think you're in *Flashdance* is just plain idiotic."

"No way! Anyway, I told J.P. not to say anything."

"And that's supposed to make me feel better? Go on, finish the story."

"Nothing happened, but he walked me to the door and his hand touched my shoulder."

"And?"

"I got all flushed. I was almost . . . excited."

"That's it, *that's* your story?"

"Yup, boring as it is."

"Excited like . . . 'turned on'?"

"That might be an overstatement, but yeah, kind of."

"And what about him?"

"What *about* him?"

"Did he seem excited too?"

"No! It was all just in my head."

"Well, don't underestimate the power of sexual energy, he must have felt something."

"I only pictured us kissing. I wasn't straddling him!"

"Maybe, but he felt something, I'm sure."

"Don't tell me that. Now I'll be embarrassed when I see him."

"Diane, unless he's the world's biggest idiot, he knew something was up from the moment you went to see him about that bogus file."

"You think so?"

"How many boyfriends did you have before Jacques?"

"I don't know."

"Come on, tell Auntie Claudine."

"One."

"*One?* Are you kidding me?"

"And I saw someone for a bit. One and a half."

"Okay, the rebound thing is really good for you. Keep your focus on the French kissing part. You're right. It's good news. Something's happening."

18

In which I conclude some things are perfect even when they're only three-quarters whole

A s CHARLOTTE PREDICTED, IT was just the two of us at the apple orchard and in the kitchen. Making the most of being on our own, we moved furniture around and repositioned artwork to hide the holes I'd made in my clumsiness and by ripping out the speakers. Some of our solutions demanded a lot of imagination.

"Is Dominic coming to dinner?"

"I don't know, he might get off late. But he'll definitely come by later."

"And how's it going with you two?"

"Not bad."

"Just 'not bad'?"

"Well, I found out he was seeing another girl last fall, and it really hurt."

"But you'd broken up."

"Only just."

"Maybe he was trying to get over you?"

"With a crazy bitch?"

"Charlotte, exes are always crazy. It's easier that way."

"No, no, seriously. She's crazy."

I was the crazy bitch in Charlene's story.

"As for the hole in the living room, what do you think about moving the big storage cabinet over it?"

Alexandre and Justin showed up at 6 p.m. on the dot with a bouquet of flowers and a bottle of wine expertly chosen to complement the flavours of the stew – vegetarian or not. As always, they were clean-shaven and elegantly dressed. Only hugging them did you smell their cologne, with its subtle blend of spices and tree bark. And as always, they wore brightly coloured shirts that could not be further from hipster trends. When they entered a room, the light took on shades of their colourful glow. Alexandre was the spitting image of his father, his good looks enhanced by a few of Jacques's most handsome features. The Love of My Life would never truly leave me.

As expected, Antoine and Malika burst in, sweaty and late. In Malika my son had found the female version of himself; someone apparently living in another dimension where Time's passing was even more accelerated. They were always in a desperate rush to get everything done, even though they had neither children, pets, nor plants. They were forever dashing in breathless and apologizing – it was never their fault – dressed as you'd expect of people who leave everything to the last minute, organization not their strong suit. All of Antoine's sentences started with "I didn't have time, but . . ." Often I wondered how to tell them that certain shirts simply needed to be ironed, but for want of finding a polite and tactful way to say as much, I never bothered. Against all odds, they'd both managed to finish their degrees, find jobs and keep them. They'd proceed in the same fashion, I imagined, when it came to having and raising kids. Already, like a good and modern grandmother, I was gearing up for the repercussions of their lack of time. I was thinking of taking up knitting.

Even though the joy of having them around almost led me to forget my unhappiness, I was reminded of it in their eager gestures, in the careful attention that so poorly disguised their desire to cheer and console me. Furthermore, nobody mentioned the missing and rearranged furniture, even though the huge storage cabinet from the hallway was now sitting smack in the middle of the living room where the couch had been, blatantly defying any decent design sense. They served me water, wine, and appetizers as if I could no longer walk; they handed me a new napkin each time I got my fingers dirty. I'm sure they'd have accompanied me to the bathroom if I'd asked. I was a victim, the mother abandoned in the family home, the one left behind. Their gaze pulled me down like leaden weights and I tried to fend it off using smiles and funny anecdotes assuring them I was fine. (My caregivers got a kick out of the leaf blower and broken arm stories.)

We were just getting ready to sit down to dinner when Dominic arrived. I never understood what Charlotte saw in him. He's kind, and devoted, but so wishy-washy you'd think he had a rubber spine. This one, no question, has plenty of time; I can't imagine him rushing anywhere. He exudes a "chill out, man" vibe anytime people talk or move too fast for him. When he moves it's as if he's trying to slow the pace of everything around him, which generally produces the opposite effect on me: he stresses me out. But since Charlotte's tastes are none of my business, I'm happy to support her tormented relationship.

Dominic is also a fierce advocate for animal rights. He works on the front lines, criss-crossing the region in his van to pick up all kinds of animals that have been reported: pigeons, dogs, snakes, lemurs, tarantulas, and more. And, when given the chance, he rails against the cruelty and barbarism of the human race. Some of his stories are utterly compelling and can even turn your stomach. His saviour complex can be charming, I'll give him that.

But I was a little alarmed when I watched him enter carrying a pet crate. What if he had something poisonous in there? Or maybe it was a lizard without a tail, a blind hamster without fur. Some beat-up animal clearly in need of help.

"Hey, Dominic."

"Hi, Di!"

I never had to ask him to call me by my first name. He'd been calling me "Di" since the second time we met.

"So what have you brought us today?"

"Wait, Mum, wait! Let me explain first."

Charlotte rushed toward the two of us, grabbed the cage, and set it down at her feet with the wire door facing in so that we were unable to see what was inside. I was quite scared but she wanted us to listen to what she had to say before we looked.

We were hardly surprised when she told the story of a cat hit by a car and taken for dead, but that by some miracle it managed to come back to life inside the garbage bag it had been tossed into. The cat tore the bag open and ran back to its owners, giving them the fright of their lives – they'd seen Stephen King's *Pet Sematary* and thought the cat some kind of zombie out to kill them. The poor creature, seriously injured, refused to leave their balcony and so they'd called to have it taken away and put down. Dominic went to pick it up, promised to euthanize it (a lie he told so the owners would be able to sleep that night), and brought it back to the shelter. The veterinarian on duty agreed to treat it, giving it a second chance at life – or was it a second series of nine lives? Science hasn't decided yet.

"He's all better now, and he's still just a baby, not even a year old. He's been neutered, dewormed, and vaccinated. And he's so sweet and cuddly, he's super soft . . ."

183

"Yaaay! A cat!"

"Let's see it!

"Take him out!"

There's no denying it, Charlotte's a clever girl. She knew the only way I'd take a cat in would be if she gave it to me in front of everyone so that I couldn't lose my temper or protest without getting bombarded by very logical counter-arguments. And the benefits of pet therapy are well documented.

Charlotte opened the door gently and the cat peeked its head out, a little frightened and overwhelmed by all the faces staring into the cage. I didn't immediately realize there was something wrong with the cat, since the grey and black of its fur obscured its movements somewhat.

"Hey! He's only got three legs!"

"Oh, poor little guy!"

"Huh?"

"Hmm . . ."

It wasn't enough for it to be a cat, it needed to be a three-legged cat. His deformity was simultaneously touching and repulsive. If I'd put him into a garbage bag believing he was dead, I wouldn't have wanted to see him get out, either. He took a few steps out of the cage and stopped, resting the remaining half of his hindquarters on the rug like a broken trinket.

"Ooooh, too cute!"

"Aw, look at him – what a beautiful cat!"

"He's kind of disgusting."

"Antoine!"

"This whole thing's weird."

"You'll see, he's super sweet."

Charlotte smiled at me and murmured, "Don't worry, I'm taking him back with me." When I asked what her roommates would think, she'd subtly averted her gaze.

I'm not allergic to cats, dogs, or anything else for that matter – what I have is a slight intolerance to leaf blowers. We never had any pets when the kids were growing up because Jacques thought they complicated things unnecessarily. He hated all that hair sticking to fabric, slipping into food, and gathering into little clumps beneath the furniture. I never put up a fight. Until Charlotte arrived, I'd actually forgotten I liked cats.

Steve – yes, that was his name, I kid you not – didn't put any one of his three legs on the ground all night. He could have lost all four and it wouldn't have changed a thing. We practically had to take numbers for a chance to hold him. The dinner slowly turned into a night of telling stories about cats. And thanks to Facebook, everyone knew – or had endured – tons of them: stories of adorable kittens with heart-shaped patches between their eyes; stories of cats giving birth in their litter boxes; of dumb cats stuck underneath the hoods of cars or in their tailpipes, and supercats that had saved a child, a woman, or a dog . . . When Malika said that a friend's grandmother had fallen down the stairs and killed two kittens – what were they doing sleeping on the basement stair rug? – I laughed until I cried, despite Charlotte's horrified expression and the tragedy of it all. Oh my daughter, the sweet, sensitive future veterinarian.

The conversation turned to how everyone was doing, the good along with the not-so-good. It had been a long time since I'd been so happy. It felt like the air I was taking in was reaching that inaccessible space at the back of my lungs for the first time in months. It would be good for jogging.

When my kids were little, I used to marvel at how they made it to the end of every day alive. They might have been hit by a car, kidnapped, injured, but no, the god of chance heard my prayers and always sent them home in one piece, if with a scratch or two. Now that they were out on their own, this visceral fear was coupled with a kind of gratitude; I knew how fabulously lucky I was to watch them get older. Twenty-five years on, gathered around the same table, the insignificant incidents of our lives continued to nourish family folklore as it gained new voices with each new couple – some, inevitably, later decoupling. I had never felt so moved at my own table. Well okay, in an ideal world there wouldn't be any cell phones, but our flaws help us better appreciate the rest.

No one mentioned Jacques or how his split from our nucleus would work. Organizing birthdays, special events, and visits would be a headache, but we'd cross that bridge when we came to it. For the moment, we weren't ready to undo the fragile balance of our new lives. The children were suffering too, of course, and they would need time to learn how to create a new well of memories and love each of their parents in separate tableaus. In order to fill Jacques's absence at dinner that night, I'd replaced his setting with bread, the butter, a vase of flowers, the bottles of wine, and a pitcher of water. I'd reclaimed the space lost when I'd dispatched his mother's buffet table. Everything was perfect.

When it was time to leave, Alexandre and Justin sandwiched me in a big hug without a word, which almost made me cry. Antoine told me he'd come take care of the yard as soon as he found the time – I didn't tell him about Mr. Nadaud, I wanted him to think I was counting on him – and Charlotte made a classic exit.

"Can I leave the cat here for a bit, just until I talk to the girls?"

"But I thought . . ."

"Well, I had to take him right away, otherwise they'd put him up for adoption. You understand."

"Of course, I get it. Leave him here until you sort things out."

"Thanks, Mum! Really, thank you! You're the best!" As a child, she used to bring home all sorts of inconvenient, often stinky, animals, some found outside – a pigeon, a cute injured mouse, a baby squirrel that had fallen out of a nest – and others friends had given her (a dog, a cat, a lizard, a ferret . . .). We'd had to trick her into getting rid of them, which always left her sad and hurt. Her decision to become a veterinarian had surprised no one.

"Dominic has food and a litter box in the truck."

"Oh, so you planned the whole thing!"

"Just say if you can't take him or don't want him. I'll figure something out."

"Like what?"

"Uh . . ."

"It's all right, sweetheart. And it's just temporary, like you said."

"That's right. I'll take him as soon as the girls say it's okay."

"Can he climb stairs?"

"Yes. It takes him a while, but he can. He gets around like a normal cat."

"Is he on any medication?"

"No, the scar healed up well. Keep an eye on it, but everything should be fine."

"He won't pee everywhere?"

"No, he's litter-trained."

"How much food do I give him?"

"There's a measuring cup in the bag. Give him one in the morning and another at night."

"And if I don't come home?"

"Oh! Do you have something to tell us?"

Her face lit up, her little hands joined in prayer. She'd have loved for me to have a life preserver. But I couldn't tell her how I'd felt when J.P. brushed against me to open the door. She'd have pitied me. And I certainly didn't want to tell her how sure I was that I'd never have a love life again.

"Sometimes I go out to dinner with Claudine."

"Oh! No worries, then just put out twice as much in the morning."

"Can he go outside?"

"No, not yet. He doesn't have all his vaccines."

"Just as well. He'd be eaten alive."

"No way, he's super smart."

They'd left my kitchen sparkling, as if I were expecting a visit from potential buyers. I'll admit, the compassion my kids show me has its advantages.

Steve the Cat followed me upstairs, lay down on the soft carpet of the bathroom while I removed my make-up, then slipped into bed with me and curled up on my pillow, purring. I inspected the fuzzy scar on his missing paw up close as he licked my forehead. The minute he snuggled into my neck, I knew I'd fallen into the trap like a sucker.

"Do you like the name Steve?" The cat blinked up at me.

"It's not a good name for a cat." More blinking.

"Let's find something else."

It took me three days to find a name. Three days during which the trap slowly closed on me: I looked forward to coming home to my three-quarters-of-a-cat.

"Cat-in-the-box. Because you've been the most wonderful surprise. What do you think?" The cat's ears twitched.

"Too bad, that's your name from now on."

He flicked his tail from side to side.

"A name with prepositional phrase. You're one lucky guy."

And that's how I started talking to animals.

• • •

"So?" said Claudine.

"I haven't opened it yet."

"Oh come on! Go get it and open it now."

"I can't. I hid it in the wall."

"What do you mean, in the wall?"

"I folded it up and pushed it through a hole in the living room wall."

"Well, pull it out!"

"I can't, the hole is about three feet up, and the envelope fell all the way down," I explained.

"You can't reach it even if you stick your arm in?"

"No. I'd have to open the whole wall."

"Then open it up. You'll have to repair that part of it anyway."

"I can't."

"Why not?"

"Because the storage cabinet is in front of the hole."

"Then move it."

"I can't do it alone. It weighs a ton."

"How'd it get there?"

"Charlotte helped me last night."

"Okay. You're a lost cause," Claudine said, throwing her hands up.

"I'm not ready. I'm not strong enough."

"Fine. We'll put the envelope on hold for now. Did you call Jacques?"

"No, I said the twenty-third."

"Aren't you curious?"

"Curious about what? The divorce?"

"Maybe that's not it."

"If he wanted to get back together, I'd know," I pointed out.

"Yeah. You're right."

If I'd told her I was still holding onto some silly hope of his return, she would have come over and smashed in the wall with her cast.

"Whatever he has to say, it's bound to just piss me off."

"You're right, there's no rush. See you tomorrow."

"You're coming back to work?"

"I can just see the files piling up on my desk. I'd rather come back while I can still catch up. Plus they called me in for some big, important meeting."

19

In which I discover that
some pits are bottomless

WHEN JOHANNE, THE SECRETARY of my department, greeted me the following morning, there
were deep vertical wrinkles running up the middle of
her forehead. The woman's facial geometry has always
impressed me.

"Someone called a few times for you. It sounded important, but I didn't want to give out your cell phone number."

"Did you get the name?"

"No. Private caller."

"A man or a woman?"

"A woman."

"Hmm. Did you recognize the voice?"

"No."

"Young or old?"

"Tough to say. Somewhere in between? She said she'd
call back."

A good handful of women hated me at the moment.
I glanced at the beige telephone in my brown, soon-to-
be-burgundy office – the goose poop had gotten only a
single vote – and, summoning Claudine's advice, I tried

to stay calm by thinking of something positive. I pictured the reconciliation that had taken place with my neighbours over a slice of apple pie; I thought about J.P.'s arms, about the family's successful stew night, and about my Cat-in-the-box.

When the telephone rang, I grabbed the receiver with such force that the base went flying across my desk. I had to pitch myself across my files so that the serpentine cord, stretched to its maximum, didn't unplug itself and cut me off.

"Diane Delaunais speaking!"

"Hello."

"*Hello!*"

"We need to talk."

"And you are . . . ?"

"Can we meet in person?"

"Uh . . . sure. When?"

"As soon as possible."

"Right now?"

"Yes, I'm free."

"I'll wait for you. I'm at my desk."

"I'd rather meet someplace else."

"Oh? That might be complicated for me."

"We can meet later, after work, if that's better."

"No, I'll figure it out. There's a little café called Café on René-Lévesque, right by my office."

"That works."

"I can be there in ten or fifteen minutes."

"Perfect."

And the woman of undetermined age hung up without taking the time to say who she was or how we'd recognize each other. She knew my name – we'd figure out the rest, I imagined.

"Johanne, I need you to take my messages. I'm stepping out to meet the woman with no name."

"The one who called this morning?"

"Yes."

"She didn't tell you her name?"

"No."

"Where are you going?"

"Over to Café. If I'm not back in half an hour, call the police."

"Do you think she's dangerous?"

"Of course not, I was kidding! It's 9:15 and we're meeting in a café full of people."

But I started to get a little spooked as I walked over to meet the mysterious woman. I had a horrible premonition that, despite everything I'd done to avoid as much, the envelope was about to open itself.

Claudine was in a meeting. I sent her a text telling her I was off to see a potential serial killer. That way, there would be at least one other person on the alert should I not make it out of Café alive. I could already see myself in a bathtub, down a kidney.

On arrival, I immediately spotted the woman in question; she was sitting up, calm and motionless, hands crossed in front of her. Unlike just about everyone else, she wasn't tapping nervously on her phone or computer. I suppose I looked like a Diane Delaunais. She gestured toward the empty seat across from her without extending me a hand to shake. Her frosty demeanour was reassuring. She wasn't looking to butter me up, she hadn't come to apologize for seducing my husband while I was focused on my quiet, happy little life. In fact, it was quite the opposite: this woman was pissed.

She let out a big sigh as she sat back down. Her lips hinted at a restrained smile I could only identify by the fine lines appearing at the corners of her eyes. She was a very attractive woman. The Kate Winslet of another generation. Certainly too old for Jacques's new taste.

"I'm Marie."

A beautiful woman with a beautiful name. Some people are just born with it.

"Diane Delaunais."

"I know."

"Do I know you?"

"Indirectly, yes."

The bomb was about to explode. Something deeply unpleasant bound us together, I could feel it. If she stopped there, my life might not fall apart; if she kept going, she would be able to finish me with a few murderous words.

"We have the same shoes."

She slid her legs out from under the table to show me her pretty blue boots.

"Oh my God! You're J.P.'s wife?"

Her lip began to tremble, her eyes welled up. "Yes."

As I flashed a full, toothy smile, something told me she was about to fall to pieces.

"What's this about?" I said.

"I got a call."

"From who?"

"Anonymous."

"Like right out of a movie." She didn't respond.

"And?" I pressed her.

"I got a call from someone who . . . who told me . . . about you and Jean-Paul."

"*What?*"

I had a brief moment of doubt, a half-second of panic. Things with J.P., if they could even be called that, hadn't moved beyond the gelatinous tubing sealed in an airtight skull, otherwise known as my brain.

"What exactly did this person say?"

"That he gave you the same pair of boots –"

"No, no! I bought these online."

"– with wine and a card."

Her hands flew up to her mouth, as if she'd burped without meaning to. Suffering was burning her stomach.

"Okay, Marie, let's straighten this mess out. You wear an 8."

She stared at me.

"So do I." I leaned towards her to explain.

"When Jean-Paul asked me where I'd bought my boots, because he liked them, I took mine off, gave them to him, and ran away. It was so dumb . . . I left the office in my socks . . ."

I lost it and started laughing like crazy. Kate Winslet stared at me like I was unhinged. All women are crazy, Marie. Every last one of us. We're all *someone's* crazy.

"Afterwards, he gave them back to me in a big shopping bag with a bottle of wine in each boot, as a thank you. He'd ordered the same ones for you! It was easy once he had the brand and model number."

"I heard you two were meeting up in secret."

"Who . . . who told you that, Marie? Can I call you Marie? Was it the same person?"

"That's not important."

"Actually, it's very important, because the person who told you that is angry with me for one reason or another and is out to make trouble. Some people are like that. It's sad, but it's true. I think I know who called you."

"Maybe, but . . ."

"I've never hung out with Jean-Paul outside of the office, not in my whole life. Nothing ever happened between us and nothing ever will, I swear on my children's lives. I'm not even sure we've ever shaken hands. Look at me, Marie. I'm forty-eight – almost forty-nine – and after twenty-five years my marriage just blew up in my face. On a good day, I take a sledgehammer to my house between swigs of white wine. I'm a total mess. Do you honestly think J.P. would fall for a woman like me?"

". . . I don't know . . ."

"Do you honestly think J.P. would want to fuck a woman like me?"

This time she let go and gave me a good, hard look. Her eyes traced the winding curve of my Roman nose, dove into the deep wrinkles of my cheeks, and slipped down under my doughy chin. I smiled when her gaze returned to my eyes, ringed with purple circles of irreparable fatigue. I hoped she wouldn't answer.

"No."

"Obviously!"

Laughter, that great popper of bubbles, freed us from a conversation far too heavy for a Monday morning. The moment was so tragicomic that I shed a few tears easily confused with what they were not. Her tears were also hiding something; they were a form of deliverance. Now that she was laughing I could see even more clearly how radiant she was.

"Have you ever doubted him before?"

"No, never."

"Well then, don't now. A guy who goes out of his way to buy you fancy Italian boots is clearly in love."

"Yeah . . ."

"Have you ever worked in a big office building full of employees confined to their desks all day long?"

"No, I teach primary school."

"Wow! A heroine, to boot!"

We said our goodbyes with a sincere handshake. I was in a hurry to get back to the office and set a few things straight.

"Any messages, Johanne?"

"So? Who was it?"

"I can't really tell you, but I swear it wasn't anything important. Let's just say there was a misunderstanding."

"Well, good. I was a little worried. No messages, but the phone's been ringing off the hook. I don't know what's going on today."

"Listen, I'm going down to see Josée and I'll be right back up."

"Josée who?"

"Josy."

"Oh?"

"That's her real name. Josée."

"Seriously?"

"Yes, ma'am."

"That's funny, I like Josée better."

I took the stairs down to the fourth floor. I had to calm down, get myself under control. In hindsight, I should have gone all the way to the basement and then come back up very, very slowly.

As was her habit, Josée greeted me with a fake smile before asking, with a friendliness as authentic as her nails, if she could help. She was wearing a magnificent eggshell jacket.

"Sure, you can help me. Is Jean-Paul around?"

"No, he's in a meeting with the execs. It shouldn't be too much longer. Do you want . . . ?"

I slammed her desk with the palm of my hand. Everything on it jumped. Her ultra-kitsch porcelain shepherd took a nosedive, pencils spilling from its faux-crystal plastic holder. Her mug had held up, so I put a finger into the coffee to check the temperature – lukewarm, perfect! – grabbed it by the handle, and threw its contents all over her. I took aim at the white jacket. The fabric, faithful collaborator it was, absorbed a lot of the liquid. The rest landed everywhere else in a delicious splash.

"Oops!"

"Aah! You're crazy!"

She began vigorously mopping at the lapels of her jacket, but the tissues disintegrated upon contact with the wet fabric. I went over to her, gritting my teeth and pointing my finger at her powdered nose.

"The next time you feel like spreading rumours, do a better job of spying!"

"You can't get away with this!"

"Oh no? You want me to tell J.P. you made an anonymous call to his wife to stab him in the back?"

"You bloody cow!"

"I hope your CV is up to date, bitch."

And with those fine words, I returned to the fifth floor whistling a Joe Dassin tune. "*Son petit pain au chocolat, aye, aye, aye!*" The day was taking a funny turn. It was not yet break time and I'd been through more emotions than I had in a year. That's the good thing about being boring: the most insignificant little thing becomes a gripping adventure.

Claudine had left me three urgent text messages demanding I come see her as quickly as possible. The big meeting had just ended. I practically ran to her office and threw open the door.

"Hey! So how's your arm feeling this morning?"

"It's fine."

"Good! Listen to this, you won't believe it: Josy called J.P.'s wife and told him we were having an affair. An affair!

I wish! That bloody cow – that's what she just called me, so I'm allowed – that bloody cow must have opened the bag with the boots before she brought it to my office, and she thought that J.P. had bought them for me! She was spying on us, that snoop! Every time I went to see him she kept thinking we were arranging little dates, you'd have to be a nutcase to make up stories like that! And you know how I found out? Check this out: J.P.'s wife called me this morning! She wanted to meet, but I didn't know it was her until I got to Café. I was so worried I'd told Johanne to call the police if I didn't make it back. It could have been dangerous – I had no idea who I was seeing. Did you get my text?"

"Yes, I did."

"I thought it would be better if two people knew. Anyway, once I got there, I recognized her easily, because we have the same boots! I realized immediately that she was his wife. The poor woman, if you'd seen her face, she was a wreck, she was completely destroyed, I'm telling you . . . Claudine, are you okay?"

"Uh-huh."

"So I cleared things up pretty fast, then I asked her if she really thought her husband would've had an affair with me . . . 'No,' she said, just like that. It was actually kind of insulting, she was basically calling me an old bag, but whatever. We straightened things out. If only you'd seen her, I swear, she's the spitting image of Kate Winslet.

She has these beautiful bright eyes . . . Are you sure you're okay?"

She was pale as a ghost. I'd never seen her like that before.

"What's going on?"

History was repeating itself. It was the second time I'd heard myself nervously ask the same question since 9 o'clock.

"Claudine?"

I knew it was serious when she got up and came over to sit beside me on the second grievance chair, the one that was used less often. Suddenly I couldn't breathe. She was about to tell me she had cancer. Or worse.

"Okay, spit it out. You're scaring me."

"Diane . . ."

"Spit it out!"

"They're restructuring."

"Who? What? They're laying you off?"

"No . . ."

"Phew! You scared me." But Diane's face remained serious.

"Who then? Me?" She nodded slowly, as if to cushion the blow.

"Me?"

"A third of all jobs. They're moving all the administrative positions to Toronto."

"A third of all jobs? That's a lot of people!"

"A lot of lives to ruin . . ."

"And you get to break the news?"

"They asked me to meet with people two at a time so it would take one week instead of two."

"Seriously?"

"I told them to fuck off."

"I'm not surprised."

"Yeah, I can get away with it because they need me to do their dirty work. They told me not to worry, they have a team of psychologists ready to help me. It's like an assembly line: I announce they're losing their jobs, they pack their boxes and then go cry to the shrink."

My life was starting to feel like the end of the world was just around the corner. I'd always thought it would arrive with a giant tsunami or fireball, something truly spectacular. But it broke over me in the most mundane form possible, in a series of cutthroat words that struck me down and made me want to vomit: *administrative restructuring*.

"Now I'll really have some free time."

"You'll get six months' severance pay."

"Fabulous."

"Diane, I don't know what to say . . ."

"There's nothing to say. I don't envy you."

"Jesus, I hate this goddamn job sometimes."

"Listen, I think I'll head home right away. I'm tired. Can you get someone to pack up my stuff ? They can figure out which file is which. The Murdoch dossier reeks of a scam."

"I'll take care of it. I'll ask Émile to do the boxes." She started to cry when she hugged me, but I couldn't summon a single tear. I was totally stunned.

"We'll still see each other, Claudine."

"I know, but . . . life's really giving you shit these days."

"You too."

I left her office and floated, weightless, across the polished concrete floor. I felt like a pumpkin that had been gutted clean, waiting to be carved. If I'd had the strength, I would have done a final bootless dash down the hallway, but I couldn't convince my arms to reach down and take them off.

I grabbed my purse, keys, and coat and left without a word. Those I passed must have waved at me, but I was already far away, numbed by torpor.

As I no longer had anything important to do, I drove around, following unfamiliar highways, exits, boulevards, and streets like somebody watching TV, absent-mindedly eating handful after handful of chips. If it hadn't been for a pressing need to pee, I might never have stopped.

When I tried to go back to the Ultramar service station I'd passed a few minutes earlier, the one plastered with neon lights and advertisements for cheap beer, I ended up lost in a sequence of numbered streets going nowhere. Yellow fields stretched out in every direction, a throwback to an earlier era. I had no idea such expanses still existed so close to the city. I pulled over and opened both passenger-side doors along the highway's gravelly shoulder to relieve myself. In front of me, scrawny ears of corn waved their brittle leaves. I hiked up my skirt, pulled down my tights, squatted, and peed as an icy breeze ruffled my backside. I tried unsuccessfully to save my pretty blue boots, now as precious as vintage wedding bands. Despite my precautions, small, steaming droplets bounced off the ground and up onto the hot leather of my boots, leaving dark spots. I hadn't done this since my last trip with Jacques to the Swiss Alps. In those days I was still flexible, perfectly able to keep my knees away from splashes. I wiped myself with my scarf and left it there, spread over the liquid rapidly absorbed by the half-frozen earth. Once I settled back into the driver's seat, I removed my boots and threw them into the ditch. We had been together long enough. They were hopelessly connected to the end of my marriage and were covered in piss. The ditch would fit them like a glove.

But for a cabin made of poorly planed boards planted in the middle of the field, there was hardly anything around. Downy sparrows perched on power lines, crows screeched, and maybe there was a three-legged cat somewhere. These open spaces told the story of my life. My soul was true to the season.

My texting icon had a little "8" in the notification bubble over it – Claudine was worried. I needed to get in touch or she'd call in the army, the police, and my entire family. I snapped out of it. I didn't particularly want my kids feeling even sorrier for me, or for Jacques to feel obliged to pull me from the depths of my despair. I typed a message to her. "Out for a drive. Need to think. Everything's okay."

"Call me, we need to talk."

"Soon, I promise."

"No, now."

"Talk soon."

I was like a tightrope walker on the high wire, focused on keeping my balance. If I talked to her right now, I was sure to fall.

Stockings are not designed to be worn without shoes. The grooves of the pedals cut into the soles of my feet like the blades of a mandoline. Numbness was setting in, and I wouldn't be able to go on much longer. In any case, the fuel gauge indicated that, against all odds, my situation was about to get a lot worse unless I got the heck out of this no-man's land. Once I reached civilization again, I'd be able to buy a pair of something or other in it didn't matter which supermarket that sold clothing and foot-wear at three-times-nothing prices made by people paid a hundred-times-nothing.

Two kilometres down the road, an old man sat rock-ing on the front porch of a small green house. He wore a quilted gabardine coat – very Canadian Tire – and a beaver hat, its tail hanging down the back of his neck. Just my luck, Daniel Boone was standing guard. I pulled off to the side of the road and lowered the window.

"Hello!"

He didn't hear me. I shouted again, louder this time.

"Hello!"

"Ah! Hello!"

"Can you tell me how to get back on the highway?"

"Pardon?"

"Which way is the highway?"

"Eh?"

I stuck my head through the window to reduce the distance between us, and bellowed.

"Can you tell me how to get back onto the highway?"

He put his hand up to his ear, but didn't stop rocking – odd activity on such a cold day. Sure, it was impolite to keep screaming from inside the car, though it was no less rude to keep rocking as he was. Whatever. I was resigned to having to leave the car and run over to his front steps. The cold and the pebbles mercilessly slashed through the tender skin of my feet. The mere idea of setting foot on grimy country soil, likely full of animal turds and spit, would have made Jacques ill.

"Hello! I'm sorry to bother you."

"Hello hello!"

"Yes, hi! I'm a little lost – can you tell me how to get back on the highway?"

"What was that?"

"I'm looking for the highway."

"You've come from where, you?"

Where had I come from? This was surreal. Physically, I was standing right in front of him, a bizarre question to ask. Metaphorically, I had no idea other than that I was caught in a tangled web of darkness.

"Where's your *shoes*?"

"Oh! I threw them into a ditch back there." I could tell he'd let it go. He didn't even bat an eye.

"Well, come on in, child. Gon' catch your death, dressed like that."

Seeing him struggle to lift himself up and walk to the door, I'd have pegged him for about a hundred. All his joints, neck included, seemed welded together. He walked like a robot prototype. Some people's bodies really hang in there.

Inside, the smell of burned butter permeated the single room of the first floor. A faint aroma wafted up from a small battered cooking pot sitting proudly on the stove in the middle of the room. There were (most likely) vegetables swirling around in it, turning in the swells of bubbling water. The walls were lined with photographs, some very old and others more recent. All of the frames were askew, as if an earthquake had just rumbled through. The little man – I was almost a good head taller than he was – didn't take off his boots as he walked over to a big wooden chest in the back of the room.

"I'll give you some slippers. I've got enough for an army, and no one around here uses 'em."

"That's okay, sir, I don't want to take your slippers."

"Since my wife died, I keep my boots on in the house."

His laugh revealed an impressive mask of wrinkles and a mouthful of blackened stubs probably only good for soft foods. A shame, since I bet the area had lots of fresh corn.

"Plus, I don't get too many visitors."

"I really can't . . ."

"What colour are you wearing?"

"What colour?"

"My wife knitted 'em in all sorts of colours – to go with her clothes she said."

"Oh. I'm wearing black."

"Black? Are you headed to a funeral?"

"Uh . . . no, I just like black."

"What was that?"

"NO, I JUST LIKE BLACK."

He was reading my lips, so I tried to over-pronounce. "Well, good. I ask, seeing as we're coming up on dying season. The Reaper does his cleaning before winter comes. So now, I'll give you these, but grab another pair from the chest if they don't fit. You must have big feet, seeing as you're so tall."

He handed me two different slippers, one green and white, the other brown, "knit to last," as my grandma would say. They had the characteristic stiffness of synthetic blends. I felt a wave of nostalgia.

"Thanks a lot, you're a lifesaver. I had a hell of a day today."

"What was that?"

"THANK YOU! I had a bad day today."

"Well then, I've got good news for you."

"Oh?"

"The soup's ready."

"Oh!"

"You must be hungry, seeing as you're lost."

I wasn't, but I didn't want to ruin the only good news of the day. He went over to the kitchen and came back with two wooden bowls and a ladle right out of a children's nursery tale. I didn't dare ask, but I'd have bet he'd whittled them from a tree himself.

"Get closer to the stove so's you can warm up."

I obeyed. I had nothing to worry about; the poor man, half-deaf and half-blind, moved at a snail's pace. Even in synthetic slippers, I could outrun him just by walking. With a steadier hand than I'd expected, he served me without even looking down at the pot. He went by the smell and the heat. And habit, I suppose.

"What did you put in your soup?" He didn't hear me.

"Here, little lady."

He handed me a bowl and sat down beside me on a chair facing the stove. I figured "seasonal vegetables," judging by a piece of parsnip I saw floating around and "little wild rodents caught in traps" by what seemed to be meat.

"Have you been living alone for a while?"

"WHAT'S THAT?"

"YOU LIVE ALONE?"

"I'm too old for you, little lady. Hah!"

"*Pfff* . . ."

"I'm joking. You're not little."

"Hah!"

"It's just me, but Mariette comes by in the evenings."

"Every day?"

"So she can get past the pearly gates. She's got a few sins she needs forgivin'."

"Don't we all."

"She's my sister. Only eighty-two, a spring chicken. A real force of nature, you wouldn't believe."

"How old are you?"

"Eh?"

"HOW OLD ARE YOU?"

"Ninety-four, they say . . . but I think that's a stretch."

If what "they" said was true, he'd been through the Great Depression, the Second World War, Elvis, the first

TV, the fall of the Berlin Wall, the Quebec flag, and a whole bunch of things we celebrate or despair of having invented. Like the leaf blower. How many loved ones had he buried? Yet there he was, calmly drinking soup directly from a bowl like any other man, using a finger to retrieve the vegetables he'd missed from the corner of his mouth. So I tried it, too. The combination of broth and overcooked vegetables, somewhere between a soup and a stew, was surprisingly delicious. If it contained squirrel meat, it was excellently cooked. Strangely, my misfortunes seemed irrelevant inside the house, as if they were waiting outside like a pack of hungry wolves. Everything that had been weighing me down, that had been smothering me only a moment before, suddenly seemed of little importance. I was drinking soup, I was wearing old mismatched slippers.

"I just lost my job."

"Do you have kids?"

"Yes, but they're all grown up. They've got their own lives. My youngest daughter is the only one still in school."

"No kids?"

I smiled and held up three fingers.

"All in good health?"

"YES, THANKS!"

"As long as the kids are healthy . . ."

"You're right . . . I LOST MY JOB TODAY."

He pulled a handkerchief from his sleeve and wiped his mouth and eyes, then blew his nose. I wondered if Mariette washed it every now and then, its colour was slightly disturbing.

"You'll find another one. Are you sick?"

"NO."

"As long as you're healthy . . ."

"BUT YOU NEED A DIPLOMA TO DO ANYTHING NOWADAYS."

"Go back to school then, you're young. Does your husband still have a job?"

"My husband left."

"Eh?"

"MY HUSBAND LEFT."

"Where'd he go?"

"Oh, somewhere far, far away . . ."

I raised my arm and made waves with my fingers to indicate the distance.

"Is he dead?"

"No. HE'S PERFECTLY HEALTHY. Maybe even too healthy."

And we ate-drank our soup, lost in our thoughts, down to the bottom of the bowl.

"To get back on the main road, drive to the junction with Route 7, turn right and take it to the end. There, turn onto the road that cuts in front of the church and follow it till you see the green sign. Church's still there, but it's not a church anymore."

"THAT'S TOO BAD."

"Good riddance! I never could stand them priests . . . Take a look at the bench over there. Picked it up when they took the church apart. Shoulda gotten a whole row for all the money I gave 'em over the years."

I wouldn't have minded staying longer, sure that he had a whole bevy of stories to tell. It would have taken hours, days even, just to go through all the pictures in their frames.

"THANK YOU FOR EVERYTHING."

"Get lost again, why dontcha. I don't get out much."

"DO YOU HAVE ANY CHILDREN?"

"Yes."

"DO THEY COME VISIT?"

He made waves with his fingers.

"I'LL BRING BACK YOUR SLIPPERS."

"No, no, they're a gift from my wife. She'da been happy to give 'em away. I've got a whole chest full."

I glanced down at my feet: I'd stretched one of them out, and the other was so big I was afraid I'd lose it with every step. The colours were awful, the material scratchy and uncomfortable. It had been ages since a gift had touched me this much.

It was only once I was back in my car that I realized we hadn't introduced ourselves. What did it matter, really?

Our names would have taught us nothing more, beyond our parents' preference for certain sounds.

I left Adélard's house – that seemed like a good name for him – recharged, as if I'd just taken a nap. When I reached the church, I pulled over to call Claudine.

"It's me!"

"Shit! How are you? Where are you?"

"Umm, in the country somewhere, hang on a sec, I see a sign . . . no, there's no name. Anyway, I'm about to get on the highway."

"What are you up to?"

"I took a long drive, got lost, and had lunch with a ninety-four-year-old man . . ."

"Have you been on Facebook?"

"What's that got to do with anything?"

"When was the last time?"

"The last time what?"

"That you were on Facebook?"

"Okay, you're serious about Facebook? I haven't been on it since my spring blitz. Why?"

"Shit."

"All right, what's going on?"

"*Shit*."

"Claudine . . ."

"You need to call Jacques."

"It isn't the twenty-third yet."

"Call him anyway."

"No! Tell me what's going on!"

"*Uggggg . . .*"

"Tell me!"

"The whore's pregnant."

The reflex was senseless, but I looked behind me to assess the possibility of turning back time, of rewinding these last few minutes and stepping once more into Adélard's cozy cocoon, suspended in time and space. But I was at the part in my own story, like Thelma and Louise when they realize they've reached the point of no return: I had to jump and face the music, to the beat or not. Holed up with Adélard, I could have sipped broth and watched the geese come and go until my body gave out, but with a smartphone that could be contacted in the remotest reaches of the country-side and spill its poison over me, I didn't stand a chance. The only thing left was to laugh.

"Can you breastfeed with fake boobs?"

"You know, I've never thought about that."

"I bet you can take them out and put them back in again."

"Maybe they can replace the silicone with bags of milk."

"With nipple-pacifiers."

"The fool posted a picture of her belly."

"You're Facebook friends?"

"Everyone is friends with everyone on all kinds of social media. You're one of only three or four people in North America who isn't."

"I forgot."

"Are you on the road?"

"Uh-huh."

"How do you feel? You sound calm."

"I'm okay."

In truth, my head was pounding so badly I had to squint to concentrate. I could see the highway ahead; I could drive as far north as I wanted, abandon my car on the side of a forgotten road somewhere, and walk to the nearest unnamed lake to examine its depths. The depths are where I'd spend the winter, hiding among the frogs.

"My kids will have a new brother or sister."

"Or both. There's an epidemic of twins going on these days."

"My children's family is growing, but not my own. It's like someone hit pause, but I'm the only one who actually stopped. I'm frozen in the background while everyone else keeps going."

"You're not on pause, Diane. You're just taking a different path."

"I was supposed to be on the same one as them."

"I know."

"It's like we're all walking in the woods together, and Jacques tells them, 'Quick! If we go this way, your mother will never see us.' And now I'm in the woods all alone . . ."

"I know."

"Philippe didn't go start another family."

"No, but my kids hide out in the woods every other week. And the week I have them, I have to look for them just the same."

I remained silent.

"Diane, you're allowed to be pissed off, but don't do anything stupid."

"I have to stop somewhere for gas. And I'm in slippers."

"Slippers?"

"Long story."

"Call me later?"

"Yeah, sure."

"You won't do anything dumb, will you?"

"I left the sledgehammer at home."

"Love you, old broad."

I filled the tank, gulped down a dishwater-flavoured coffee, and drove straight home. I didn't know what else to do.

After pulling into the driveway, I turned off the engine and sat there behind the wheel. I let the pain wash slowly over me, like a tide pulled gently by the movement of the stars. Let it come. I no longer had the strength to run away. I opened my mouth and let the moans, wails, and shouts escape. I clung to the wheel, my whole body a sound box, and screamed with all the strength I could muster. I was screaming like someone being tortured, desperately trying to kill the sickness inside. Once I'd emptied my lungs, I took a deep breath and started all over again, trying to push my cries farther, louder, stronger. I wanted the windshield to shatter, the car to explode. When I felt my vocal cords started to tire, I redoubled my efforts, determined to stretch them until they burst. Rage fuelled rage; unending pain ran down my neck in little rivulets. My innards would end up slipping out of my body like a string of sausages. I would purge myself until there was nothing left of me but skin. I would die.

I was well on my way down a fatal path of self-eviscera-tion when I felt a hand close around my arm.

"Diane! Diane!"

Tattoo Guy from the construction site down the street was crouched next to me, having opened the car door, head lowered so he could look up at me.

"You're okay, you're okay . . ."

I was gasping for air as if I'd just run a marathon. My face was covered in tears, snot, drool – anything a body produces when it goes into panic mode. The bloated feeling of my eyes and mouth told me my face was swollen. The veins in my temples were pounding to the rhythm of my broken heart.

"Are you hurt anywhere?"

My hand swept the air from left to right. Apart from a sore throat and a headache – and the numbness of my feet – there was nothing to report.

"Can I take you to the hospital?"

"No."

"A clinic?"

"No."

"Can I call anyone for you?"

"No."

"Do you think you can get out of the car?"

"No."

"Okay, I'll take care of it. Want a tissue?" It must be worse than I thought.

"Yes."

"KLEENEX, GUYS! NO AMBULANCE, SHE JUST WANTS KLEENEX!"

Mrs. Nadaud came running out with a damp facecloth and a box of tissues, free hand clasped around her jacket collar. She reminded me of my mother, who'd been dead for so long that I'd lost the habit of thinking about her in difficult times. I whispered "Mum," just to feel the effect of the word on my tongue. The urge to cry sprung up like a geyser, coming at me all the way from my distant thirties. I blew my nose hard enough to bury my sobs. *Mum*.

Despite the carnage of my face, Tattoo Guy came a few inches closer. I could feel the heat coming off his body. I hadn't noticed that I was completely frozen.

"Would you like to go home?"

I glanced past his head to my house, anchoring his suggestion in reality. My house was behind him, and light years away from me.

"Uh-huh."

"All right then, put your arms around my neck, I'll take you in."

"No . . ."

"*Yes*. You can't stay here."

Before I could get a word in, he slipped his arm of steel under my legs and swept me up. Fortunately, I hadn't peed myself. The day I sunk to my lowest point, I was carried across the doorstep like a young bride.

"Nice slippers."

He deposited me in an armchair in the living room and knelt down in front of me. If it hadn't been so much like Jacques's proposal, classic to the core, I'd have found it endearing.

"There must be someone you want to call?"

"Not yet."

"I don't think I should leave you alone."

"I'm tired. I'm just so tired . . ."

"Bad news really takes it out of you."

"Yeah."

"Okay, I need to get back to work. But I'm not far – let me know if you need anything."

"I'll yell if I need you."

His lips pulled back and he let out a little laugh, then leaned in closer and hugged me like an old friend. He held me so tight and for such a long time that I was able to close my eyes and rest my head on his shoulder in delicious abandon. Enfolded in his magnificent arms, my woes suddenly seemed negligible. The fragments of my shattered soul settled one by one in the folds of his neck, a store of pain to be swept away. My body drank up his warmth, his calm, his gentleness.

If it hadn't been for the woman with flaming hair keeping watch underneath his plaid jacket, we might have kissed. His prickly cheek gently grazed mine before he pulled away. Our lips almost touched. I took everything he offered.

After he left, Cat-in-the-box came out of hiding and snuggled up against my neck. He nibbled my earring and then fell back into a deep sleep full of nervous twitches. After a thousand therapeutic caresses, I gratefully nodded off with him.

· · ·

When I opened my eyes, Claudine was standing above me with a giant platter of sushi, wearing the sad smile she reserved for the worst days.

"Come on, we're celebrating your new life. I brought an excellent bottle of temporary solution."

I squinted up at her.

"I know you don't feel like it, but it'll be good for you. Don't move, I'll take care of everything!"

"Claudine?"

"Yeah?"

"I lost my rebound."

"Oh, sweetie . . ."

20

In which I see myself in the mirror

MY HAIRDRESSER WAS RUNNING late. I sat down on her Louis XVI sofa and pretended, as usual, to be looking for a new style or colour in one of the fashion magazines randomly scattered across the coffee table. It hardly mattered. Whatever bold decisions I'd made in the moments before seeing the scissors invariably vanished the second I sat down in Sabrina's chair. But my determination to embrace current trends crumbled in the face of my boring nature, manifested right down to my choice of hairstyle.

"So what are we doing today?"

"The usual."

The girl Sabrina had just finished with – the one responsible for the delay – was raving ecstatically about the pink fade now visible, after lots of bleaching and colouring, in the last ten inches of her hair.

"This is exactly what I wanted! I love it! My friends are going to be so jealous. Mum's on her way over to pay you."

In the back, a woman as round as a marble was talking to Eve, the other stylist.

"I want to change it up. I look a bit severe. Do you think my face would seem a little longer if we added a touch of colour on the sides?"

"You don't have the length for that. We can play a little with the cut to get the effect you want."

"But what if we put a little red here, on top? Wouldn't that look nice?"

The woman had managed to convince herself that a few coloured highlights would make her look several kilos lighter. Human nature lives by hope – it's one of our greatest talents. We feed off illusions that help us escape, if only for a moment, the harshness of reality.

"That might look nice, but we'd have to bleach first to get the right colour."

"Is that absolutely necessary?"

"If you want a nice, bright red, then you don't really have a choice."

"All right then, let's do it!"

She giggled happily, excited at the transformation she was about to undergo, counting on a little colour to boost her look and morale. Her pudgy little fingers danced with glee in the air.

I noticed my reflection in the large mirror at the back. Grey roots; the calculated pose of an older woman. I was there for the illusion, just like everyone else.

"Hey, Diane, so you want the usual?"

"Actually, I'd like to go back to my natural colour."

"This is too dark for you?"

"No, my *real* natural colour."

"I don't understand."

"Grey."

"Are you serious?"

"I'm serious."

She looked at me in the mirror, trying to figure out what was going on. I could understand. Most women try to hide their age, not throw themselves headlong at it. But she wouldn't give me a lecture. Sabrina asks few questions, does good work, does it fast, and doesn't tell me her life story.

"I'll give you grey highlights and try to make them as close to your natural colour as possible. That way the grey will come in gradually. We'll do touch-ups every two or three months. In two years, you'll be all grey."

"I'd rather cut it off right away."

"What did you have in mind?"

"A chin-length bob. That way the grey will grow in quicker, no?"

"That would look amazing, but I need you to promise me you won't regret it."

She swivelled the chair around and looked me in the eyes, her eyebrows raised.

"I promise."

"A few months ago, I had a client come in here asking for a cut like Jennifer Lawrence."

"I don't know who that is."

"It doesn't matter. She had hair halfway down her back and she wanted me to cut it short."

"Oh!"

"So I did. It looked amazing – everyone in the salon thought so. We took pictures of her before she left and everything. But she came back a week later and yelled at me!"

"What? Why?"

"She regretted it. Said she was feeling down when she came in and that I should have tried to stop her."

"You poor thing."

"I don't do refunds and I can't glue back hair once it's cut."

"What did you do?"

"I made her sit down and cool off, then I showed her how to style it with mousse and everything. Silly girl, she had no clue how to do it. It looked awful, all flattened to her head. You've got to style a cut like that. I gave her some sculpting gel."

"That was nice of you."

"And I told her to leave me the dates of her period for next time."

"Hah! Don't worry about me, I'm sure this is what I want."

"Good. Okay, let's do it."

Two and a half hours later, I took my first selfie with Sabrina, who showed me how to upload a picture to Facebook. Everyone thought I looked great. Likes, hearts, and positive comments ("Nice!" "I love it!") popped up from everywhere. Nobody would do a double-take when they saw me. Friends and acquaintances could discuss my new look behind my back and speculate on my mental state. That's the advantage of social media: whether it's a breakup, a baby, or a haircut, the initial shock is mediated by the screen.

"Do you know a good real estate agent? A really nice one?" I asked Sabrina.

She pointed to a stack of business cards next to the register.

"He's a friend. Super-professional and super-sweet, not your average sleazeball."

"Thanks. Can I say you gave me his name?"

"Sure, he's one of my brother's friends."

"I met with one last week and it was awful. Just the smell of him was unbearable."

"You'll see, this guy's a real gem. Damn, you look good. I don't know why we didn't think of this sooner!"

My hair stylist does on the outside what my therapist does on the inside: helps me feel beautiful.

When the mother of the girl with pink highlights showed up, she was taken aback.

"What's going on? What did you do?"

"We gave her a nice fade . . . wait, you didn't know?"

"Tell me you're kidding."

"Oh my God!"

"What colour is that?"

"Pink."

"Pink? Are you serious?"

"It's all the rage right now!"

"And how much does this hot new look cost?"

"Sit down first."

"No. No, no, no. How much?"

"Well, we had to bleach it twice and then do three rounds of highlights . . ."

The mother shot the stylist a look.

"Two hundred and forty-five dollars," the stylist said nervously.

"*What?* Christ, she's got nerve. It's like she thinks I shit money. I'd never even spend that on myself!"

I looked in the mirror, and the woman staring back at me had magnificent grey highlights she'd paid for with her severance package. She knew full well that it made her look her age.

She didn't seem unhappy.

. . .

I needed to see the agent arrive. Say what you will about not judging a book by its cover – I think the cover gives you a very good idea of what's inside.

He showed up at the time we'd agreed on, punctual as a private investigator in a mud-streaked Subaru Outback.

Without meaning to, I noticed that his wheels weren't mounted on mags (Antoine once told me guys who are into cars see them as an extension of themselves – they'll never go out in public without mags). He was wearing dark jeans and a navy polo, no jacket or dress shoes. It was a casual look, maybe too casual – I seemed overdressed next to him. And he was younger than I was expecting. In his late thirties, maybe. Bushy eyebrows. If he'd let his hair grow, he would have had a monk's crown.

"Hello! Ms. Delaunais?"

"Stéphane?"

"Yes."

"Do you mind if we use first names?"

We sat on the back deck, in chairs I'd carefully dried off. I needed to have some idea who I was dealing with before letting him cast a professional eye on my interior. I'd done the same thing with my dentist.

He pulled out a pad of lined paper and an HB pencil like the kind I used to buy the kids for school. The agent I'd met with the previous week had made my head swim with digital presentations and visual touring software before we'd even agreed to work together. I should have sent him packing after his first "ma'am." But I had a good feeling about this man, with his unbleached teeth and student's face. He looked me in the eye with a serious expression.

"Can I ask you a personal question?"

"No."

He suppressed an awkward laugh. We'd stick to the essentials, that would be enough.

"No problem. Excuse me."

"I want to sell my house because I want to move. That's it."

I must have seemed idiotic, but I didn't care. I had no desire to tell him about my marital problems. No more him than anyone else, for that matter. If buyers wanted to know why I was selling, he could say what I'd just told him – which, after all, was the truth. I wanted to move. My motivations were nobody's business.

"Perfect. Are you in a rush to sell, Ms. Delaunais?"

"Diane."

"Excuse me. Are you in a rush to sell, Diane?"

"It depends on what that means."

"Do you have an ideal date in mind?"

"I don't want to be here for Christmas."

In my worst nightmares, I pictured myself alone at the head of a ridiculously long table, no one else around, staring down at a camel-sized turkey sitting in its juice. The TV was on to keep me company and *Miracle on 34th Street* was playing in all its faded glory.

"All right, then you have three options: (a) 'I've got all the time in the world,' (b) 'I want to sell, but at asking price,' and (c), the more aggressive, 'I've got to get the hell out of here.'"

"How does the aggressive option work?"

"I get a team to come in and stage the house, we list it a tad below market price to bring out the offers and maybe even start a bidding war, and I offer the other agent a good cut. It might only take a weekend."

"And what do I do?"

"Nothing. Other than think about the move."

"I like it."

"I imagine that you . . . that you've already started looking at other places?"

"No, this is my first step. Sabrina gave me your name yesterday."

"Nice hair, by the way."

"Thank you."

"I could find you something pretty fast."

"I don't really know what I'm looking for."

"I can create a buyer's profile for you with the things you already know you're looking for, like the number of bedrooms you want, the area you're interested in, the price . . ."

"In town."

"You sure? There are some nice houses for sale in Montcalm . . ."

"In Limoilou."

"Limoilou? That area is mostly apartments . . ."

"That's right, an apartment."

After a week of minor touch-ups that included repairing the holes in the walls and putting a guardrail around the deck, my house was in great shape. I'd only supervised the work done in the living room to make sure the cursed envelope remained inside its wall prison and nobody found it accidentally. It would rot between two layers of Gyproc, choking in its mire of secrets. The load-bearing wall would stay until the end of time, when it would be demolished along with the house in a great apocalyptic wave caused by glaciers melting or Hell's inferno. In any case, long after I was dead.

The staging team arrived in their stilettos to "emphasize the house's charm." At the risk of speaking to something I know nothing about, I highly doubt that a fake planter placed above a kitchen island will convince anyone to buy a house – mine or anybody else's. So when I saw them walk in carrying a basket of plastic fruit and artificial tulips, I took it as my cue to leave, though not before making my own little proposal.

"What if we made muffins for the open house?" They paid no attention.

"The smell of fresh baking . . ." Still no response, as they carried on setting up.

"Oh forget it, it was just an idea."

The aggressive option worked almost too well. The following week, Stéphane announced that we'd received three offers. With muffins, we'd have had a half-dozen.

"When do you want to hear the offers?"

"I don't think I have the nerves for that."

"I can deal with the agents and present the offers to you afterwards."

"Unless . . ."

Stéphane hated the idea, but I didn't want to have to deal with the beseeching looks from agents trying to persuade me their client "needed" my house and how it was a "great product" – so I hid in the pantry. I was comfortably installed in a soft chair so as not to make any noise when the first agent came in.

She showed up late: strike one.

"Hey, Stéphane, how's life? You just keep on getting better looking! Listen, I have an unbelievable offer that'll knock your socks off, just you wait. Your client's a real weirdo, though. Did she think I'd bite? (*Strike two.*) Well anyway, my clients are really nervous – they loved the house, though I don't really understand why. (*Strike three.*) Me, I find Cape Cods really depressing (*You're out!*)," and so on and so on. She called him "honey" every second sentence, using the word to connect disjointed thoughts ranging from technical considerations of the sale to unsolicited information about her personal life. It had been scarcely ten minutes and already we knew practically every detail of her last breakup. And that she'd just put in an IUD.

The second agent entered the room as quietly as a mouse and spoke so softly I could hardly make out what she was saying. In an effort to get closer to the keyhole,

I knocked over a few potted tomato plants sitting on the ground.

"Something's moving in there."

"No, it's the plumbing."

"It sounds more like a small animal."

"It's an old house. The heat just kicked in and the wood is reacting to it."

"We need to know if there's a pest problem."

"The place is fine, Carole. I promise."

"Can we just open the door to make sure?"

"Oh, look at that, Bertrand's already here! So when would your clients want to take possession?"

The Bertrand in question was wearing tap shoes or something similar. I could feel his presence, his weight, his smell. I pictured his tanned skin, dyed hair, heavy watch.

"Steph, my man! It's been ages since we've made a deal!"

"Yes, it has. Have a seat."

"You won't believe the offer I've got for you, Steph! Big money."

"I'm listening."

"I'm sure we'll be able to work something out."

"My client's going to look everything over with a clear head."

"Listen, Steph, I've got a great price for you. My clients are sitting by the phone, they're just waiting for the final figure."

"What do you mean?"

"You're a real card, Steph!"

"I don't understand."

"No?"

"No."

"I know you do, but I'll lay it out for you anyway."

"Don't bother, Bertrand. I'm not playing games. Your offer?"

"No, not my offer, Steph, *yours*. Your offer is our offer."

"Don't give me that preacher shit. You've got three minutes."

"I only need ten seconds. Give me your number and it's done."

"You know I can report you for that."

"Easy, Steph! Calm down, man . . ."

"You've got thirty seconds left."

He scribbled down a number before leaving in a huff. Like so many others, he didn't care one bit about the rules of the game. An inquiry into real estate brokerage would reveal no more than what every other commission does: some win by cheating. We encounter genuine honesty far less than we do a little deception. The systems in place are like the human body, imperfect and functional.

In the end, I went with the offer from the loudmouth who didn't like my house. Her buyers liked it, and they made up for her. Plus, she was representing a family with four kids. All the rooms, including the basement, would be filled with games, laughter, tears, whispered confidences, dreams, and scraped knees. They wanted a forever home, just as we had done twenty-five years earlier. I hated myself for the cynical little laugh that slipped out. My old house, like me, was still licking its wounds and it would benefit from a shot of new blood. Imagining it bursting with life was probably the only way I could tear myself away.

The kids came by to collect the furniture they needed or wanted to keep. They fastidiously packed up childhood keepsakes that would enhance their lives – or basements. I'd planned it so that, come moving day, everyone arrived at the same time and it felt like we were all changing houses together. It's what kept me, in the moment, from falling apart. I did tear up a little when Alexandre told me his memories were in his head, not the house. I'd rarely seen him so shaken, my sensitive boy. Whether we liked it or not, from now on our family history would be split into the before and the after. I took my sweet firstborn into my arms and rocked him, standing up. That's all I could do for the two of us. The reassuring words that, all my life, had come so naturally were out of reach. I was overwhelmed by the pain and incapable of extending a hand to pull us out from under it.

I came back the next day, alone, and cried for a long time in front of my beautiful old Cape Cod. The life I'd created for myself was losing its final moorings. The last traces of before were being uprooted. My loved ones, every single one of them, had left to make a new life. Without me. They were all building stories in places that didn't involve me anymore. I felt lost, abandoned, like the wounded soldier you have to leave behind to save your own skin.

I needed to start a new story, a new life. I needed to press "reset."

Charlotte had let me keep Cat-in-the-box.

• • •

When she saw my new hairdo, my therapist could tell we were meeting for the last time. Paradoxically, I decided to stop treatment once I better understood her role in it. I'd entered her office as if it were a confessional, believing that through penitence – paying a church tithe or an hourly fee amounted to the same thing – I'd free myself from the dark clouds by disgorging them into the woman-sewer. I liked to think she used yoga to shake off the abundance of secrets she harboured in the same way that priests use sacramental wine to unburden themselves of the indignities they shouldered in the name of the Holy Father. But I'd misunderstood: my therapist was a mirror, not a dumping ground. And thanks to her I'd ended up seeing, between two shadows, the woman I was still able to be. This hadn't been the plan when I'd married, of course. But I had learned, since, that life's unpredictable nature is one of its best qualities. Nobody gets on a ship thinking it will sink. That said, ships do sink. The ocean floor is littered with wreckage slowly being consumed by sea flora and fauna. But with each passing day more ships, more majestic yachts, take to the sea. It's understandable; the ocean is so beautiful. Love, like the sea, is so worth the risk.

"Jacques always protected me. Once he leapt out of the car in the middle of winter with a crowbar to defend me against some idiot I'd cut off who was out for my blood. *Jeez* . . . he picked up the tiny pieces of me when my mum died, that's hard . . . he helped me recover from 'our' pregnancies, like he used to say . . . he never wanted me to suffer, he wouldn't let anyone hurt me. Now I'm going through the biggest heartbreak of my life, I'm suffering more than I ever thought possible, and he's doing nothing, he's watching me bleed and not doing a thing, he's the one who plunged the knife in . . . All the time I've been imagining he was going to come back, that he would take me in his arms and tell me he'd made a mistake . . ."

"And now?"

"He's not coming back."

"Does that scare you?"

"I've never been more terrified in my life."

21

In which I knit, walk, and dance

"WHO'RE YOU?"

"My name's Diane, what's yours?"

"Simon."

"Where do you live, Simon?"

"In my house."

He glared at me with big, mean eyes. His finger was pointing to the end of the lane.

"You're alone?" I asked him.

"The dwarfs, where are they?"

"What dwarfs?"

"The ones that were here!"

"You lost some dwarfs?"

"No!"

"How old are you, Simon?"

"Five-an'a-half."

"Are you in kindergarten?"

"Yeah."

"Do your parents know you're here?"

"*SI-MON!*"

A tall girl came running over, hair flying, fists clenched. She didn't look especially happy.

"Simon! You're not allowed to cross the street alone! Mum's so mad! Everyone's been looking for you. Come on, let's go. You're in real trouble now!"

"I think he's looking for his dwarfs."

"Oh, hello!"

"Hello!"

"There used to be dwarfs here."

"Real ones?"

"No, garden gnomes. There was a garden full of gnomes and all kinds of gnome accessories . . ."

"And a wheelbarrow," added Simon.

"Yeah, there were houses, a well, wheelbarrows, a windmill, mushrooms, all sorts of things."

"Where'd it all go?"

"It's gone, Simon! Madame Nardella moved away."

"I just bought this duplex with a friend of mine. I live on the second floor."

"You're lucky, it's brand new. They tore down the house that used to be here. It was a bungalow."

"Yeah, the contractor told me."

"We have to go. My mum's waiting."

"You're so lucky to have such a nice big sister!"

"No, I'm not."

"There are five of us and he's the only boy, so he doesn't think he's so lucky."

"Five? And you all have the same mother?"

"Yeah."

"Zazie, look, a cat!"

"*Whoa!* A three-legged cat!"

"That's Steve, my cat. I call him Cat-in the-box. He follows me around everywhere."

"Where's his leg?"

"He had an accident."

"Oh no!"

"It's okay, he went to the doctor and now he's doing really well. He runs everywhere and loves the back lane. He's got tons of friends here!"

I thought it best not to mention the several birds and two mice he'd brought home since we moved in.

"I got a cat, too."

"Oh yeah? What's his name?"

"Potato-B."

"Potato-bee? That's a funny name!"

"It's because Potato-A died."

"Save it for later, Simon. We've really got to go. Mum's waiting."

"But I wanna pet it!"

"Another time."

"What's your name?"

"Isabelle. But everyone calls me Zazie."

"I'm Diane."

"Hi, Diane."

I chose the second floor so I'd have more light. I set up two beautiful guest rooms. Claudine moved into the first floor. Her daughters have a room in the basement. Everyone is happy. Laurie loves being in the city, so close to her college. Adèle was kicked out of her private school for a whole packet of reasons – any one of which, according to her principal, would have sufficed. And while it was humiliating – there's that old saying, the apple not falling far from the tree – Claudine was happy with the way things worked out.

"The new school doesn't cost a dime and it's right around the corner. No more drop-offs and pick-ups for Ms. Can't-Move-Her-Ass."

Claudine believes, a little naïvely, that the new school is going to pull her daughter out of her vegetative torpor. I truly hope she's right. And as every second week I see Adèle almost every day, the two of us are doing our best to get her into gear. Her doctor has confirmed she's in perfect working order, biologically speaking. We've just got to get the machine going.

Alexandre refused to be his future baby brother's godfather. He thinks that even for a man in a mid-life crisis, his father was pushing it by asking. It's bad, I know, but that did me good. My son went to bat for me, and I'm grateful. I'll be capable of generosity later, once we've gotten over the pain.

I gave up running. Life's given me enough reasons to suffer; I don't see the need to add another. Not for now, at least. For the same reason, I asked for a divorce without waiting and without fuss. I cashed in what the mercies of marriage – and the services of a good lawyer – determined was my due, all the while ignoring my ex-mother-in-law's entreaties. Marriage does have its advantages: I'm in no rush to find a job. And I've taken up knitting.

On the other hand, every day I lace up my sneakers and walk kilometres to get reacquainted with the neighbourhood I grew up in. The aged trees are still there, the old baseball stadium too, along with a few schools and the hairdresser-barbershop on the corner of 3rd Avenue. Little cafés, specialty food stores, and artisan boutiques keep popping up all over the place. And the balconies and alleys are still the centre of the universe for locals. On hot nights you can hear the clinking of glasses, bottles, and dishes. I close my eyes and drink in this music – me, the rhythmically challenged one. The great hiccup of my separation brought me here, to revisit childhood memories almost intact.

These new spaces in my life have taught me a terrific lesson: my children are not Jacques. What I see when I look at them is in no way tainted by the fact of his being their father. Quite the opposite, actually. They embody what I most loved about him, and certainly I'll never deny the feelings I had for him. Trying to put into words the love I have for my kids is a dizzying exercise. I love them immeasurably. All things considered, nothing else matters.

In the gardening section of the local hardware store, soon to be transformed into a mess of snow shovels, I came across a nice collection of garden gnomes. If someone had told me that some day I'd purchase a garden gnome for anything other than a joke, I would have never believed it. They're so kitsch they're almost cute. My middle-aged heart trembled a moment.

"They're really popular these days, ma'am. I was out of stock almost all summer. Those ones came in at the end of the season, that's why I still got some left."

"They're not on sale?"

"No, miss! They're going up three bucks in the spring, and they'll fly off the shelves like hot cakes."

Far be it from me to be fashionable. I just want to make Simon smile the next time he comes by with one of his sisters.

I chose a gnome pushing a little wheelbarrow.

• • •

"J.P. says hi."

"Uh-oh! J.P. the hottie! Give him a kiss for me."

"You bet I will."

"You look funny."

"Here, open this up."

"Champagne? No!"

"Oh yes!"

"What happened?"

"You won't believe it."

"What?"

"I finally got a cheque from Philippe!"

"No way! Party time!"

Friday nights are reserved for Claudine and me. We crack open a bottle or two of "temporary solution" and solve a few of the world's problems over takeout from the corner shop. No cooking, no dishes, no guilt; we share our big, messy lives, the ones our grandmothers never knew. Once we've warmed up enough, we turn on the music and dance in our socks on the varnished living room floor. My body moves to its own beat and I let it: I'm free. Laurie tells me I have a "unique" way of dancing. For a boring wife with such an ordinary story, that's a pretty great compliment.

MARIE-RENÉE LAVOIE was born in 1974 in Limoilou, near Quebec City. She is the author of three novels, including *Mister Roger and Me*, which won ICI RadioCanada's "Battle of the Books" – the Quebec equivalent of "Canada Reads" – and the Archambault Prize. She lives in Quebec City, where she teaches literature.

ARIELLE AARONSON left her native New Jersey in 2007 to pursue a diploma in Translation Studies at Concordia University in Montreal. She holds an M.A. in Second Language Education from McGill University and has spent the past few years teaching English in the Montreal public school system and creating educational material for second-language learners. This is her first translation for Arachnide.

WELBECK

PUBLISHING GROUP

Love books? Join the club.

Sign up and choose your preferred genres to receive tailored news, deals, extracts, author interviews and more about your next favourite read.

From heart-racing thrillers to award-winning historical fiction, through to must-read music tomes, beautiful picture books and delightful gift ideas, Welbeck is proud to publish titles that suit every taste.

bit.ly/welbeckpublishing

WELBECK

ANDRE DEUTSCH

MORTIMER

MORTIMER

WELBECK